"THERE'S A MAN IN MY BED!"

Allison Cairns-Whiteacre unlocked the door to her flat and stepped inside. How different her flat was from the home she'd just left. Ingersall Hall was a palace of over one hundred rooms, whereas the flat was one small room, lit by a single bare bulb. Still, this was wartime, and the place was within a short walk to her job as a chauffeur with the Allied Officers' motor pool.

Suddenly, Allison stopped and stared at her bed, then gasped aloud. There was a strange man in her bed!

"What are you doing here?" Allison asked in an angry and frightened voice.

The man moaned something in his sleep and turned over.

"Will you answer me?" Allison said again. "Answer me at once, sir, or I shall be forced to call the police."

The man opened his eyes slowly, looked up and frowned at the pretty young Englishwoman.

"Who are you?" he asked. "Who are you and what are you doing in here?"

"Who am *I*?" Allison said. "I come home and find you in my bed and you ask who I am. You're a Yank, aren't you? It would take a Yank to have this much gall. Now, answer me: who are *you?*"

"I'm Martin Holt, USAF, and I'm sleeping here—or I was sleeping here until you woke me. You've a very loud way about you in the morning . . ."

The War-Torn
by Robert Vaughan

THE EMBATTLED AND THE BOLD

Robert Vaughan

A DELL/EMERALD RELEASE
FROM JAMES A. BRYANS BOOKS

Published by
Dell Publishing Co., Inc.
1 Dag Hammarskjold Plaza
New York, New York 10017

Dell ® TM 681510, Dell Publishing Co., Inc.

ISBN: 0-440-02298-3

Printed in the United States of America

First printing—August 1983

This book is dedicated to
my wife, Ruth Ellen.

During the soft hours
of early morning light
comes the time I like the best.

I say goodby to
the retreating night
and hold you to my breast.

And the sun
comes into the room
and the moment goes away.

But it doesn't cause
too much gloom,
because you're mine for another day.

PROLOGUE

The air of the Wet Mouse pub was heavy with smoke and the smell of damp wool. It was illuminated by red lights, not for atmosphere, but because its clientele was composed of R.A.F. fliers, and the red lights protected their night vision.

Like attracts like, and when the American fliers learned of the Wet Mouse, they began to frequent the establishment as often as the R.A.F. Here, the rivalries and bickering of the Allied commands were put aside in the brotherhood of the sky. Their kinship was forged at 25,000 feet, where the blood which was shed on the alclad skin of the airplanes coagulated in the sub-zero temperatures with equal ease, be it British or American. It was cemented by bursting flak and exploding fuel tanks, and by lungs which ruptured for the lack of oxygen. In a unique way, known only to these men, this brotherhood extended to the German fliers as well, for even their deadliest enemies were brothers in the crucible of air warfare.

In a corner of the room nearest the dart board, and beneath a poster which depicted Hitler cupping his ear to listen to loose talk, there was a table no different from any of the others, except to the people who had claimed it as "their" table. Allison Cairns-Whiteacre was sitting at that table, waiting for Martin Holt, the American flier who normally shared it with her. Allison's bitters had not been touched, but the ashtray was nearly full of bent cigarette butts, stained red in the same shade as the attractive young woman's lipstick. It was obvious to anyone who looked at Allison that she was nervous, and even as she ground one cigarette out, she fished through her purse for another. As she put the new cigarette to her lips, a lighter flashed beneath it.

"Cheer up, Allison, everything will be fine. You'll see. Why, hell, this was nothing but a milk run."

Allison looked up, past the flaming lighter, into the face of its owner. She recognized him as George Thomas, an American friend of Martin's. George's brown tunic was hanging unbuttoned and his wings gleamed red in the house lights. For an instant, they looked as if they were blood-soaked, and the color frightened Allison. She closed her eyes to blot out the image.

"Is anything wrong?" George asked.

"No," Allison said. When she opened her eyes, the illusion had vanished, with the slight change of angle between the wings and the light. She held her cigarette in the flame and drew on it. As the smoke drifted up from the lighted cigarette, she spoke again.

"You'd think I would be used to this by now, wouldn't you? After all, I did sweat out the big ones."

George snapped his lighter shut and set it on the table, a subtle indication that he was going to join her. He sat down, then reached across the table and squeezed her hand.

"Go ahead and sweat it out," he said. "Believe me, we all do. There's no need to feel self-conscious about it. If you ask me, Martin is just damn lucky to have someone sweating it out for him."

Allison returned the squeeze.

"Where is he now?" she asked.

George smiled. "Allison, you know I can't tell you that."

"No, I don't mean where is his target. I mean in the mission. Has he encountered fighters yet? Has he run into flak?"

George looked at his watch. "By now, they are

already on the way home. That means no more fighters. The Germans have so few fighters left that they save them for the bombers on the way in, not on the way out. They lost most of their air cover last month, when they tried their last big push.''

"But they have jets,'' Allison said. "Martin told me about the jets.''

"Yeah,'' George said. "They do have jets, and they do scare the hell out of you. But they don't have that many of them, and their time on-station is so short, due to their fuel consumption, that they don't stay around long enough to do much damage.''

A British airman joined Allison and George then, and his blue tunic, like George's brown jacket, hung open. Though the uniform regulations of both services dictated that the jackets be buttoned at all times, it was a badge of membership in the brotherhood of the Airmen of the Wet Mouse that the jackets be unbuttoned the moment the men stepped inside.

"Hello, Allison, George. Is Martin out?''

"Yes,'' said George.

The British airman, a flight officer by the name of Douglas Handley, patted Allison's hand. "Not to worry, love, it's a piece of cake now. He'll be all right. Jerry couldn't get to Martin when he had the wherewithal to do it. He's not about to get through to him now.''

"Did you go out last night, Doug?" George asked.

"Took a bit of a jaunt, yes," Douglas answered. "If you ask me, Jerry is through. There are no cities remaining that we haven't bombed into the Stone Age. Butcher Harris has had it his way, all right. He said he didn't want to leave two bricks standing together, and that's what we've bloody well done. Germany is one big rubble pile."

"It has to be having some effect, doesn't it?" George asked. "Surely the war can't go on much longer, can it?"

Douglas laughed quietly. "George, my friend, this is January 5, in the year of our Lord, 1945. You've barely been in it now, for four years. We are going on our seventh."

"I know," George said. "I hope we never catch up with you."

"Well, the only way you could do that would be for us to drop out of the fighting for a while, wouldn't it?" Douglas teased.

"Yeah, I guess so," George said.

"You know what's wrong with the bloody Yanks, don't you?" a loud, rather obnoxious voice called from across the room.

Allison, George, and Douglas looked toward the speaker. He wasn't an airman. In fact, he wasn't even a serviceman. He was dressed in civilian tweeds and a bowler hat. He was a rather portly man, with a Churchillian rotundness and a Churchillian cigar. There, however, the similarity stopped, for he had none of the Churchillian charm or command. Despite the fact that he was speaking very loudly, few people were paying any attention to him.

"I say," he said again. "Didn't anyone hear my question? Would you like to know what is wrong with the bloody Yanks?"

He, like his question, was totally ignored by everyone in the pub.

"The trouble with the Yanks is, they are over-paid, over-sexed, and *over-here.*" He laughed uproariously, spraying pieces of cigar butt from his flapping lips.

No one joined him in his laughter, and when he realized that he was laughing alone, he tried to explain the joke.

"Don't you get it?" he asked. "They are *over*-paid, *over*-sexed and *over*-here. It's quite a good joke, actually."

"I say, would someone be a good fellow and show this rather obnoxious gentleman out?" one of the British airmen said. Two other British airmen walked up to the portly civilian and began politely, but firmly to escort him toward the door.

" 'Ere, now, what is this?" the civilian blustered, as the two men took hold of him. "Would you mind tellin' me what's goin' on? I've not finished m' ale! I paid good money for it."

"Buy yourself another," one of the airmen said,

putting a folded bill in the man's tweed jacket pocket.

"Yes, but do do it elsewhere, won't you, my good man?" the other airman said.

Once the civilian was hustled through the door, the two airmen turned back toward the crowded pub, rubbing thir hands together, as if they had just completed a rather distasteful task. The clientele, silent during the civilian's attempt to joke, now laughed in loud appreciation.

"Okay, guys, let's hear it for the Limeys," an American shouted, and all the Americans cheered loudly.

"Barkeep," another American called. "A round of cheer, for everyone here."

"Would you listen to the bleedin' poet?" one of the airmen said, as he and the others stepped up to the bar to get their drinks. The bartender kept a careful tab so the Americans could be presented with the bill.

Douglas returned to the table carrying three drinks, and he gave one to George and Allison.

"Drink up, Allison," George invited. "It'll do you good."

"I don't know," Doug said, smiling. "If I were you, I'd be keeping my wits about me. Who knows what nefarious scheme this fellow has in mind? He may be trying to get you tipsy, you know, and it could only be for some immoral purpose."

"Oh!" George said, pretending shock. "Do you

really think *I* would do something like that? Don't forget, she is the girlfriend of one of my own countrymen. I would never go so far as to try and make time behind the back of one of my own countrymen. She is perfectly safe with me. You do know that you are perfectly safe with me, don't you, Allison?''

"Yes," Allison said. "I know that I am safe with you."

"You trust me completely, right?"

"Completely," Allison said, smiling at his intensity.

"Good, good," George said, and fixed what he supposed to be a lecherous smile upon his face. "Now that we have that established, do you suppose I could get you to come over to my room in the BOQ? I have some etchings I think you would find interesting."

Allison laughed good-naturedly at George's antics, and the laughter was good for her, because it got her mind off the fact that Martin Holt was, at this very moment, on a mission over Germany.

Doug joined in the banter, and, mercifully, the time began to pass. Finally, an American stepped just inside the door of the Wet Mouse, and the noise in the pub subsided considerably with his entrance, for he was Major Stallings, the Air Operations Officer for the 605th Heavy Bombardment Group. He would have word of Martin's mission status.

14

"George," Allison said, putting her hand on his. "It's Major Stallings."

George twisted around in his chair to look toward the operations officer.

"They are coming back," Stallings said, and several of the Americans in the pub stood and buttoned their jackets, because they were going to the field to watch the B-17's return. George was one of the first to stand.

"George?" Allison said. She looked at him with pleading eyes. "George, can I come with you?"

"Allison, if you think it's rough here," George said, "you should be out there." He looked at Allison, and saw that he did not convince her. "Listen, there will be planes coming in without engines, or with holes blown in them big enough to drive a truck through."

"Please?" Allison asked.

George sighed and ran his hand through his hair.

"All right," he said. "Come on. I may regret this, but I can't turn you down when you look like that."

"Thanks," Allison said.

"I have a jeep outside," George said.

Allison followed George outside, where half a dozen jeeps were already beginning to pull away from the curb as other Americans were hurrying out to Wimbleshoe Air Base. Allison climbed into the front seat, and a couple of officers who had asked George for a ride climbed into the back.

This was a reversal of position for Allison, for she worked as a driver in the Allied Officers' Motor Pool, and normally it was she who provided the transportation. She was off duty now, though, and dependent upon George's good graces to get out to Wimbleshoe. At least her pass would allow her through the gates.

Wimbleshoe Air Base was named for Wimbleshoe Creek, a swiftly flowing stream which ran nearby. As a little girl, Allison had loved Wimbleshoe, for it was a place of picnics and lawn parties. Now the name Wimbleshoe had taken on a totally different meaning to her, for it was an American air base from which B-17's flew daily missions against the Germans. Captain Martin Holt, her lover and her purpose for living, flew one of those B-17's.

The gate guard checked Allison's pass, then let the jeep through. George drove right out to the tarmac and parked. They sat there, waiting, searching the eastern sky.

It was cold and gray, and Allison slipped further down into her coat. Her nose was very cold and it felt as if it wanted to run. Near the jeep, a line of vehicles began to assemble. There were, in addition to the other jeeps, fire engines, wreckers and ambulances. Behind the line of vehicles, remaining discreetly out of plain sight, though ominously present, were the hearses which would remove the bodies from the planes.

A couple of G.I.s were throwing a peculiarly shaped ball back and forth. It resembled a rugby ball, but Allison had learned from Martin that it was an American football. When she asked him once if he had ever played American football, he had answered, "some," and the other Americans who were with them at the time had laughed.

"He was just All-American, that's all," one of them had said.

Allison wasn't certain what the term "All American" meant, but she realized that it must be an achievement of some merit. Every time one of the Americans mentioned it, it was with respect.

The fire-engine drivers started their engines, and, one after another, they coughed and growled as they whirred into life. Soon a dozen motors idled noisily.

"There they are," George said, pointing into the grey sky.

At firt Allison thought George was mistaken, because she saw nothing. Then she saw tiny dots growing larger until they became great, four-engined bombers.

"There are four missing," one of the soldiers who had been throwing the ball said to his companion. "See, there are only sixty."

"Sixty? That's all we sent out," his companion replied.

"No, we sent out sixty-four," the first soldier said.

"Are you sure?"

"Look, I filled out the up-chart," the soldier insisted. "I damned well know how many planes we sent out on this mission. We sent out sixty-four, and there are only sixty coming back. We are missing four. The question is, which four?"

"Jesus, I thought this was supposed to be a milk run," the other soldier said.

"Yeah? Well, there ain't no Santy-Claus," the first one replied.

"Oh, George, what if . . ." Allison started to say, but she couldn't force the words out. She bit her lip in nervous fear.

"Don't start worrying about it until you have to," George said.

"I can't help it," Allison said. "I can't get my mind off it."

"Think of something else," George suggested. "Think of anything. How about the first time you ever met Martin? Can you remember anything about that?"

"Yes," Allison said. "Yes, I can remember everything, as clearly as if it happened yesterday."

A jeep drove by the line then, having just come from the tower.

"We just got the report," one of the men in the jeep called. "No stragglers. The four planes missing went down."

"Oh," Allison said, putting her hand to her mouth. She felt the bile of fear leap to her throat.

"Tell me about it," George urged.

He reached out and took Allison's hand. "Go on, kid," he said softly. "Tell me about how you met Martin."

"I found him in my bed," Allison said, and she laughed, despite the terrible tension of the moment as she thought of how she had first met the man she loved. "I remember how the day began. . . ."

1

It was the morning of June 5th, 1943, and Allison was at Ingersall Hall. She enjoyed any opportunity to visit her parents' home, as her duties as driver for the Allied Officers' Motor Pool kept her in London most of the time.

Allison poured herself a cup of tea from a silver service set which had a history nearly as long as the house itself, and sat on a rose velvet chair to drink it. She was alone in the great room, a room which had hosted kings and queens; princes of the church and commerce, and once, or so the legend had it, gave shelter to a young writer by the name of William Shakespeare.

"Ingersall Hall," the peerage book read, "is a fine Jacobean pile started in 1608 and completed with the addition of a 'new' wing in 1777. It is located 130 miles from London, and is said to be the exact geographical center of England. It is the home of the Earl of Dunleigh, General Sir Percival Chetwynd Alexander Cairns-Whiteacre. The earldom was created June 15, 1448. The family name, Cairns-Whiteacre, was hyphenated at the creation of the earldom by royal recognition of the legitimate claim of Arthur Cairns to being the bastard son of Henry Alton Whiteacre. The Whiteacre name is mentioned in the *Domesday Book*, the list of England's landowners in 1086."

To those interested in such things, Ingersall Hall was history. To Allison, Ingersall Hall was home.

As Allison sat at the long table which could easily seat forty diners. Its size served to accent the fact that she was alone.

Allison was a very pretty girl, with soft chestnut hair, deep blue eyes, and a clear rose-petal complexion. She was very slender, though with curves womanly enough to make the uniform she wore fill out in all the correct places. The uniform was olive drab in color, with a shoulder flash of red, white and blue. The flash read, "Allied Officers' Motor Pool."

Allison heard the click of shoes on the floor, and she looked up as her mother entered the room. Lady Anne Cairns-Whiteacre had the dignified look of one who was a lady by birth, title and deportment. She had much of the beauty of her three daughters, and, in maturity, she was even more lovely than she had been as a young woman. It was easy to see why she had been the toast of English society, and had enjoyed equal popularity on the continent. She took her role as the wife of an earl seriously, and was head of the British Ladies' Hospital Brigade as well as a member of the executive staff of the First Aid Nursing Yeomanry. Indeed, Lady Anne was as active in the war effort as her husband or any of her children.

"Allison, dear, are you having only tea?" Lady Anne asked. She started for the buffet to pick up a small silver bell.

"Really, mother, this is all I want," Allison said, holding up her hand to stop her mother from ringing the bell.

"But you've a long day ahead of you, dear," her mother scolded. "You can't go far on tea."

"I'll eat a good lunch," Allison said.

"Do you promise me?"

"I promise."

"I worry so about all you girls," Lady Anne said. "Karen works hour after hour as a skywatch volunteer, Midge kills herself in the hospital, and you drive all hours of the day and night. I'm sure not a one of you are paying the slightest bit of attention to your health."

"Yes we are, Mother. Really, we are," Allison said. She finished the tea, and then, because her mother was still frowning in disapproval, she took a sweetroll from a tray on the buffet. "I do wish Father would come on," she said.

"Don't worry, Allison, the war will wait for me," General Sir Percival Cairns-Whiteacre said, coming into the room at that precise moment. He kissed Lady Anne lightly on the cheek, then kissed his daughter. "Is that your only breakfast?" he asked her.

"I've already spoken to her about it, Percival," Lady Anne said. "I received only a promise that she would eat a good lunch. You will see that she does, won't you, dear?"

"Of course," the General said. "We'll eat American today. We are going to visit an American camp."

"What a surprise," Allison said sarcastically. "My day just wouldn't be complete without seeing an American."

"I thought my own daughter would understand and appreciate the Americans," Percival said. "Especially in view of my position."

As the Earl of Dunleigh, Sir Percival had been born with a colonel's commission in the Royal Guards, as had every Earl of Dunleigh before him. The military ranks weren't always ceremonial either, for Percival had commanded a regiment during World War I and his father had been in the Boer War. One of his ancestors played a major role in the defeat of Napolean at Waterloo, so military duty came as naturally as the rank itself.

"I'm sure you are right, Father," Allison said. "It is good that the Americans have come, and I know that it means we are no longer alone against Hitler. But you should *see* the Americans. They have taken over London and turned it into . . . into Brooklyn," she said, trying to come up with a typical American city. She laughed. "Oh, and have you heard this song?

> *Dear old England's not the same,*
> *The dreaded invasion, yes it came,*
> *But no, it's not the savage Hun,*
> *It's the goddamned Yankee army's come."*

Allison finished the song with a laugh, and her father joined her, though her mother expressed shock at the language.

"I suppose you learned that language from the Americans?"

"It's just a song, Mother," Allison said. She picked up her hat and started for the door, still smiling. "I'll bring the car around for you, if you are ready," she called back to her father.

"Yes," Percival said. "I'm ready."

The General turned to his wife as Allison left for the car.

"Will you be here when we return tonight?"

"I think so," Lady Anne said. "Why did you think otherwise?"

"I never know when you will have a conducting exercise," Percival said.

"Well, thank goodness I don't have one today," she said.

Percival put his hand on his wife's shoulder. "I know you find them distasteful, Anne," he said. "But war is a distasteful business, and we must all do what we can."

"I'm glad the girls don't know," Anne said. "I think my job would be much harder if they knew."

"Someday I would like them to know," Percival said. "Someday I would like them to be as proud of you as I." At that moment, Allison honked the horn, and the General, after kissing his wife again, went outside to the car.

It was an American car, a Packard, painted light brown, with the lights muzzled so that they were little more than cat's eyes. It aggravated Allison that the steering wheel was on the wrong side. The Americans insisted upon putting the steering wheel on the left, and Allison had a hard time adjusting to it. She would have preferred an English car, but the motor pool, like so many other facilities, was now totally dependent upon American equipment.

The relationship between the Americans and the English had been born of necessity and had developed into rather a macabre partnership. America was literally buying time with British blood. British soldiers had fought and died in France and North Africa while the huge American industrial machine was producing war materials. British sailors died at sea, while American merchant ships brought the material over to English shores. And, finally, British airmen were dying in the skies over Europe, while the Americans were building up their Air Force.

The procedure was working well, for England was being turned into a military warehouse. Allison's father was in charge of procurement for Allied bases, and he told Allison that so far he had acquired more than seventy million square feet of storage space. That did not include the space for air bases and army camps. The Americans had brought in more than fifty thousand vehicles as well as airplanes, ammunition, gasoline, motor oil, lumber, brooms, dried eggs, talcum powder, coffee, chocolate and an unending supply of American cigarettes.

Allison guided the Packard down a quiet country road, and, passing through the dappled shadows cast by the sun through the trees, she was able to see graphic evidence of the build-up of supplies. Along each side of the road, shielded by steel arches, stood pile upon pile of artillery shells. She shuddered at what she saw, because one bomb from a German plane could set off the entire road.

"Father, do you really think it wise to store these shells in this manner?" Allison asked.

Sir Percival chuckled. "Believe me, my dear, I have flown over this area a dozen times, trying to find where we stored the shells, and they can't be seen. They are shielded by the trees and by the steel arches. It looks like nothing more than a roadside culvert, so don't worry about anything. The Germans will never know they are here."

"But they are right out in the open," Allison said. "A spy could see them."

"There really is no defense against a determined espionage agent," her father answered. "The only thing we can do is defend against the most obvious danger, and in this case, it is German reconnaissance planes."

"I suppose you're right," Allison said. She smiled. "After all, General Morgan did think enough of you to put you in charge of such things."

"That he did, girl, that he did," Sir Percival replied. "I hope I am equal to the responsibility he has put upon me."

"You are more than equal," Allison said. "No general in all of England could do a better job than the job you are doing."

Percival laughed. "You will be sure to mention that to General Morgan the next time you see him, won't you?"

"Of course," Allison replied with a chuckle.

"Do you think General Morgan will be placed in command of the invasion, when it comes?"

"No," Percival said.

"You don't think so? But hasn't he been doing his job well enough?"

"He's been doing an excellent job," Percival said.

"Oh, I know, it will be General Montgomery, won't it? After all, he's made such a name for himself in Africa. I don't propose to be an authority on such matters, but it would seem to me that General Morgan would be a better choice, since he has been with it from the beginning."

"Well, perhaps you should tell Churchill about General Morgan, right after you tell Morgan about me," Percival teased.

Allison laughed. "Touché," she said. "I do rattle on, don't I?"

"If one can't rattle on within one's own family, where can one rattle?" Percival asked. "But the truth is, the supreme commander will probably be an American."

Allison laughed. "An American? One of the Piccadilly warriors? I do hope they find one who is sober."

"I'm quite serious, Allison."

Allison looked across toward her father. Her passengers normally rode in the back seat, but because this particular passenger was her father, he was riding in front.

"But you can't be serious," Allison said. Then, as she studied his face, she added, "Good lord, you *are* serious."

"It has to be that way," he said. "After all, the Americans will be providing most of the troops, and, lord knows, they are supplying most of the equipment. I feel it is the only way to ensure their enthusiastic and whole-hearted support for the operation."

"You mean you agree with the decision?"

"Agree with it? I'm strongly recommending it."

"But what about our chaps? Will they go along with it? I mean fighting for a commander who isn't British?"

"Oh, as far as the average Tommy goes, he won't know the difference. He'll still be with his own regiment, among his own friends, commanded by his own officers. It's just that in the coordination of events, someone has to chair the committee, and as most of the equipment and men to be coordinated will be American, the chair should be filled by an American."

"Who will it be?" Allison asked. "I hope none of the generals I've carried in my car so far. I certainly saw nothing inspiring in any of them."

Percival chuckled. "Heavens, dear, I don't have the foggiest. I would rather suspect it will be General Marshall. He is their top-ranking soldier, and I wouldn't think they would want to give this job to anyone else. After all, it would be rather an

30

insult to give the job to a low-ranking general, don't you think?''

"I would think so, yes," Allison said. "But I have nearly given up trying to understand the Americans."

"Has your experience with them been that bad?" he asked. "Look here, my dear, are you suggesting that . . . that is, has any American officer made any indecent. . . .?"

Allison laughed and put her hand on her father's hand. "Oh, Father, how sweet! I do believe you are ready to go forth and do battle for my honor."

"Don't you think your honor is worth doing battle for?" Percival asked, a little stung by his daughter's laughter.

"I would hope it is worth doing battle for," she said. "But believe me, Father, it has not been impugned. Here I've been so harsh in my assessment of the Americans—it is no wonder I've given you cause to wonder. It isn't that, it's just that I think the Americans are a swaggering, boastful, loud-talking, beer-drinking breed which I find most irritating."

Percival laughed aloud. "Well, I must say you summed them up rather well. But don't forget, they are, in a sense, our kinsmen, and if ever there was a need for family to come together, that need is now."

"Well, here we are," Allison said, turning off the road and heading toward a white gate. An

American military policeman stepped out toward the car, holding his hand out to stop them. Even in that gesture, military though it was, there seemed to be an implied swagger.

"This is *General* Sir Cairns-Whiteacre," Allison said, accenting the word General for the American M.P.'s benefit. It was effective, because the M.P. snapped to attention and rendered a hand salute.

"Go right on through, General," the M.P. said. "You are expected, sir."

"Thank you," Percival said, returning the salute.

"Look how he holds his hand when he salutes," Allison said under her breath as they drove away. "They can't salute any better than they can say the word *leftenant*."

Allison drove through the makeshift base until she reached the headquarters building. It was an easy building to find, as it was the only permanent structure on the entire base. Everything else was made of canvas or corrugated tin.

An American general and an English brigadier were standing in front of the building. They saluted as Allison drove up. Percival got out of the car and returned the salute. When he noted the puzzled expressions on their faces, he realized they were wondering why he rode in the front seat. He smiled as Allison got out of the car and walked around.

"My dear, you have made an old man's ride

quite pleasant," he said, and he kissed her. When the puzzled looks turned to shock, Percival laughed. "Gentlemen, may I present my daughter?"

Now the American general and the English brigadier smiled, as much in relief as in amusement, and both saluted Allison and greeted her warmly.

"General Whiteacre, we have just unloaded some new American carbines," the American general said. "Would you care to come to the target range and fire a few rounds?"

"I would be delighted," Percival answered. "Show me where."

"It's right this way," the American general said.

At that moment, a distant sound of rolling thunder began to grow louder, and one of the Americans who had been throwing a ball back and forth shouted, "Here come the B-17's!"

Allison looked up as the bombers flew over. There were more than one hundred of them, huge four-engined jobs, sending down an avalanche of sound which deafened those on the ground and caused their stomachs to shake. Wave after wave of the planes flew over as they headed for the airbase at Wimbleshoe, about thirty miles north.

"Jeez, lookit that one," Allison heard someone say, and she looked up to see one of the bombers trailing smoke. Two of its engines weren't turning.

"How 'bout that one? Half of its tail is shot away."

"I wonder how many they lost today?"

"A bunch of 'em," another voice answered.

The planes passed on over and the camp grew quieter. It became so quiet that the conversation in a nearby tent could be heard, quite easily, by Allison and those who were standing near her.

"Hey," some unseen soldier said. "Did you see what was drivin' that Limey General? You think she's not buckin' for a promotion?"

"What do you mean?" By some freak of sonic physics, the entire conversation was as audible as if they had been standing right next to the generals.

"I mean the way he was ridin' in the front seat with her 'n all. I tell you what, I'd like to have a general's star for just one hour. I'd show that good lookin' heifer somethin'."

"The only thing you could show her, you dumb son-of-a-bitch, is a chancre sore on your pecker." There was general laughter from the others in the tent.

"Lieutenant," the American general hissed to his aide. "Find out who that is and put him on report."

"Yes sir," the lieutenant answered. He took a small notebook and a pencil out of his pocket and started off in the direction of the tent.

"No need to put anyone on report," Sir Percival intervened. "Just ask him if he could make his false assumptions in a quieter voice."

34

with you. You'd be some kind of a hustler. You could make a fortune."

Percival laughed. "It's a fine weapon," he said. "It's been more years than I care to remember since I last shot in competition, but this weapon made it easy."

The rest of the visit to the American camp was less eventful. There were the normal inspections, a parade, a mess hall lunch and a review of the troops, then Allison and her father left the camp and returned to Ingersall Hall.

"Allison, you will be staying the night with us, won't you?" Percival asked.

"I don't know," Allison said. "I really should be getting back to London. I have to go back on duty tomorrow afternoon and I have a few things I need to do before then." She laughed. "I've really become the ordinary working girl, Father. I do my own laundry and everything."

"Good for you," Percival said. "And the others? Do they ever say anything?"

"What others?"

"The girls who work with you. Do they ever say anything about Lady Allison Cairns-Whiteacre driving a car and working in an ordinary job?"

"Most of them don't know that much about me," Allison said. "And those who do seem to take it in stride."

"I can't help but think this is a good experience for you," Percival said. "I'm most thankful we were born fortunate enough to have the advantages of an earldom, but for every door that opens, another is shut. This is your opportunity to open some of those doors which would otherwise remain shut and to see and experience life at large.''

''Mother certainly doesn't seem to be able to escape her identity, does she?'' Allison said. ''She seems to be in all the newspapers and magazines.''

''Well, your mother is a most attractive woman and beloved by all of England,'' the General explained. ''Her high degree of visibility ensures volunteers for the hospitals.''

''I know,'' Allison said. ''I'm not complaining. I was just making an observation.''

''Of course, neither of your sisters are making any effort to conceal their identity. Both of them have been working and contributing to the war effort, too, but their fellow workers have always been aware of their station. I'm sure they aren't having the same learning experiences as you.''

''I know,'' Allison said. She laughed dryly. ''I doubt that either of them has had to wash their own underthings.''

''Really, Allison, is it necessary to discuss such things in public?'' Percival scolded.

Allison laughed again. ''I would hardly consider it public to discuss such things with my own father. However, if it embarrasses you to think of your daughters in underthings, perhaps we could do without them.''

40

"No," Percival said quickly. "No, we'll just leave things as they are." He joined her laughter.

"It has been a lovely holiday, Father. I'm so glad you were able to arrange it."

"Why don't you spend the night here and get an early start in the morning?" Percival asked. "I really don't like you driving at night with just blackout lights to guide you."

Allison reached around to massage the back of her neck. "I suppose I should be very noble and say I must go on," she said. "But my own bed sounds awfully good to me right now. I think I'll just take you up on that and stay over."

"Good, good," Sir Percival Cairns-Whiteacre said. "Your mother will be very pleased."

2

The Allied Officers' Motor Pool was located very near Piccadilly Circus, and Allison's flat was within walking distance. That made it convenient for her, but it also meant that she would have to walk by the notorious Rainbow Corner, a very large American service club.

There were always dozens of American service-men standing in front of the club and leaning against the walls, light-poles, fire hydrants and kiosks. They made wisecracks and laughed at strange jokes only they could understand. They danced to their own improvised music, which they called jitterbug, and, most distressing of all to

Allison, they yelled and whistled at passing girls. Allison found that particularly disturbing, for whenever she walked through the area, morning or evening, day or night, she felt as if she were being forced to run a gauntlet of abuse and harrassment.

When Allison turned the corner toward the service club, she took a deep breath. It seemed as if the crowd this morning was larger than ever. Where did they all come from? Why were they out here so early? She had the idea that many of them may not have gone home the night before. That meant they must have spent the entire night standing in front of the Rainbow Corner.

"Oh my god, I'm in love!" One soldier suddenly shouted, and he clasped his hands over his heart in exaggerated mime.

"You aren't in love, you're in heat," another soldier answered.

"It's the same thing," the first one insisted. "Do you see what I mean? Check out the babe coming toward us now. Look at that doll, would you? All that meat and no potatoes."

"Hubba, hubba, honey!"

"Hey, baby, how'd you like to mop up a little soda-pop rickey, huh? We could paint this ole London town red."

"Shake it, but don't break it, honey!"

"Don't listen to these guys, doll-baby. They'll lead you into nothin' but trouble. Now me, I'm serious. I want to get married. What do you say? I can start that ole allotment check rollin' your way, first thing in the morning.''

Everyone laughed, and Allison's cheeks flamed red. She stared straight ahead and forced herself not to pay any attention to the men, but to concentrate only on getting past them.

"Hey, sweetheart! Have you heard about the new panties on the market? One Yank and they're off! Get it? One *Yank!*" There was more laughter.

There were two heavily painted women, obviously prostitutes, at the far end of the building, and they seemed to be enjoying Allison's discomfort as much as the soldiers were enjoying the banter. One of them stepped out toward her as she approached.

"Be a good girl, would you, dearie?" she said. "Go somewhere else next time, and give a poor working girl a chance."

"Yeah, dearie," the other one said. "Go somewhere else. You're bad for our business." They laughed as raucously as any of the soldiers.

Allison looked at the women and started to reply, but she feared that a reply, any reply, would just be playing into their hands. She bit her tongue and continued. Mercifully, the harrassment ended as soon as she had passed the building, and now it was but a short distance to her flat.

The flat was on the fourth floor of an old hotel called the Cecil House. The Cecil House was a narrow building, its heavy door wide and black with a brass knocker right in the middle. A narrow

45

stairway was tucked up against one wall and covered with a worn carpet which may have been maroon at one time. Now it was gray and, where the inner weave showed through, brown.

Allison let herself in and started up the stairs. The door to the apartment manager's office opened, and Mrs. Chestnut stuck her head out.

"Oh, it's you, dearie," Mrs. Chestnut said. "I thought it might be Miss Standridge. I've a few words to have with that one, I do."

"If I see Elaine, I'll tell her you are looking for her," Allison said.

"It won't do no good," the old woman said. "Fac' is, it'll just warn her 'n she'll be better able to dodge me. But I'll catch up to her, 'n when I do, why we'll have a set-to. You can mark m' words on that. D'you know what she had the cheek to do las' night? She let a man inter her flat!"

Allison had to smile, despite herself. It was well known that Elaine Standridge managed to sneak men into her room. As a very pretty girl who worked inside the Rainbow Corner, she had ample opportunity to meet men—and few inclinations to turn down their offers.

"I don't know," Elaine once told Allison. "They are all so handsome and they are all so far away from home, and who knows if they will ever get back home? Somehow I feel that it is my duty to offer those poor men some comfort."

"But do you have to offer them the comfort of your bed?" Allison asked.

"Why not?" Elaine had answered. "I don't know of a more comfortable place."

Allison liked Elaine despite her rather 'loose' ways, and she and the other girls of Cecil House often conspired to keep Elaine out of trouble. They found ways to cover for her with Mrs. Chestnut whenever they could.

"I'm sure you are mistaken, Mrs. Chestnut," Allison said. "Elaine knows that you don't allow men in the rooms. I know she would check with you before doing such a thing."

"I tell you, there *was* a man in here," Mrs. Chestnut said. "I saw him going up the stairs last night. But by the time I got up there, he was gone. I knocked on Miss Standridge's door, but she didn't answer. So I thought I would just let things be until this mornin', sort of give her enough rope 'n let her hang herself, if you get my meanin'. But when I went up this mornin' and she still didn't answer, why I just let myself into her room with the pass key, 'n then seen that I was too late. She 'n the man with her was both gone. But I'll catch her yet."

Mrs. Chestnut closed the door and Allison climbed the steps on up to her apartment. She had left Ingersall Hall at 3:30 in the morning, driven through the pre-dawn darkness and arrived in London at 6:30. It was now nearly seven. She didn't have to go to work until three that afternoon, and it felt good to have most of the day to relax, do some laundry and find some time to read.

Allison fished in her bag for her key, unlocked the door and stepped inside. She was struck by how different her flat was from Ingersall Hall, as she always was when she returned from a visit home. Her parents' house was a palace of over one hundred rooms, whereas her flat was but one room, lit by a single bare bulb which hung from a frayed cord. She had a small ice-box, a hot plate, a table and three chairs. There was a sink against the wall, but the loo was down the hall. She had made a feeble attempt to brighten up the room with a bowl of wax fruit and a basket of silk flowers, but it had done little to relieve the drabness.

Allison happened to glance toward her bed, and she gasped aloud.

There was a strange man in her bed!

"Who are you?" she asked in an angry and frightened voice.

The man pulled the cover over his head.

"What are you doing in my bed?" Allison asked, more shrilly than before.

The man moaned something in his sleep and turned over. It sounded as if he said the word 'feather.' Yes, he'd said, "Feather engine number two."

"Will you answer me?" Allison said again.

"Answer me at once, sir, or I shall be forced to call the police."

The stranger in her bed opened his eyes slowly. He looked up at Allison, then frowned in confusion.

"Who are you?" he asked. "Who are you and what are you doing here?"

Allison couldn't believe the audacity of the man. How could he have the nerve to ask her who *she* was, and what *she* was doing here, when *he* was sleeping in *her* bed? And yet, even as the thought came to her, she realized by his accent that he was an American, and that answered the question for her. He had the cheek to do such a thing because he was an American.

"Who am *I*?" Allison asked. "I come home and find you in my bed, and you ask who am I? You're a Yank, aren't you? It would take a Yank to have this much gall. Now, shall I go to the police, or will you tell me who you are and what you are doing here?"

"I'm Martin Holt, and I'm sleeping here. At least I *was* sleeping—until you woke me up. You've a very loud way about you in the morning."

"I can *see* that you are sleeping here," Allison said, beginning to lose her patience. "I want to know *why* you are sleeping here."

"The person who rents this room told me I could sleep here. See, she even gave me the key."

Martin got out of bed then, and started toward

49

the table where he had left his key, change and billfold.

Allison looked at him, and, even though she was angry, she couldn't help but notice that he was an exceptionally handsome and well-built young man. He had wide shoulders, a broad chest, a flat stomach and sinewy legs. She could make such an appraisal because he was standing before her in only a pair of shorts. The front of his shorts gaped open slightly, and she saw a dark bush of hair. She looked away in quick embarrassment.

"What are you doing?" she asked. "You're naked."

"What? Oh, no, I'm not naked, I still have on my skivvies," Martin answered distractedly. He began shoving coins around until he found the key, then turned and held it up triumphantly. "Ah, here it is, right here. So you see? I'm not an unauthorized intruder."

"Where did you get that key?" Allison demanded.

"From Elaine Standridge. I met her at the U.S.O. last night and didn't have a place to stay. She told me she was going to the country overnight, and she was generous enough to allow me the use of her room."

So, this was the man Mrs. Chestnut had seen going up the stairs last night, Allison thought. But he hadn't been in Elaine's room, he'd been in her's. That was why Mrs. Chestnut couldn't find him when she searched Elaine's flat. If the old woman only knew! Allison, unable to help herself, laughed out loud.

The man seemed puzzled by her laughter, but grateful for it. "Well," he said. "I'm glad to have you laughing, instead of yelling at me."

"I might have known," Allison said. She noticed on his shirt the captain's bars of his rank. "Captain, did you bother to read the number on the key?"

The man looked at the key, then read the number aloud.

"It's 404," he said.

"Precisely my point."

The man looked at the key, then at the woman, and the look of confusion on his face showed that he had no idea what she was talking about.

"This is 402," she explained.

"This is 402? But I don't understand, the key fitted the latch perfectly."

"Half the latch keys fit half the doors," Allison said. "This is a very old hotel, Captain. Security obviously isn't what it should be."

"Then who are you?" Martin asked.

"My name is Allison Cairns," Allison said. "I am Elaine's neighbor."

"I'm Martin Holt," Martin said, starting toward Allison with his hand extended.

Allison looked away, smiling. "I absolutely refuse to shake the hand of every naked stranger I find in my bed."

"I told you, I'm not naked," Martin said. He grinned broadly. "And now that you know my name, I'm no longer a stranger."

"Please," Allison said, looking away from him. "Do get dressed."

"Okay," Martin said easily. He reached for his clothes. "Say, I'm awfully sorry about this. Could I buy you breakfast, as a sort of apology?"

Allison saw that Martin's right knee was scarred and misshapen, and she felt a sudden sense of pity for the young man.

"Is it very painful?" she asked, pointing to the knee.

"Sometimes," Martin admitted. He laughed. "At least I always know when it's going to rain."

"I'm sorry," Allison said. "It seems such a shame to have to spend the rest of your life with a wound like that. The quiet tragedy of this war is the hundreds of thousands of wounded who will bear scars and pain for the rest of their lives."

"It's part of the price," Martin said. "Now, how about that breakfast? Will you go with me?"

"Really, I can't," Allison said. "But I do thank you for—"

"Please," Martin interrupted. "I, uh, don't get around all that well on this knee, you know, and I don't know of any place close where I can eat. You'd be doing me a great favor if you would help me find a restaurant or a coffee shop."

"Perhaps I could direct you to a nice place," Allison offered.

"No," Martin said. He laughed, and his boyish grin was so infectious that Allison found herself drawn to him, almost against her will.

"I'm terrible at directions," Martin explained. "If I didn't have a navigator in the plane with me, I'd never find my way anywhere. You are just going to have to go with me. Unless, of course, you are prejudiced against Americans."

Allison laughed now. "I must confess that you have hit upon a truth. I am prejudiced against Americans."

"Then, in the interest of better Anglo-American relations, you are just going to have to get over that," Martin said. "After all, I managed to overcome my anti-British prejudice."

"You were prejudiced against the English? But how could *anyone* be prejudiced against us?" Allison asked.

"Oh, you think prejudice goes only one way? Let me tell you why you are prejudiced against Americans, and you tell me if I'm right."

"Very well," Allison said. "Why am I prejudiced?"

"You consider all Americans ill-bred boors, wasteful and obnoxious creatures disrespectful of tradition and custom, womanizers, and," Martin smiled broadly, "they're totally incapable of speaking the King's English. Am I on track?"

"Yes," Allison said. "You are remarkably accurate. But do go on. Why should you stop there?"

"Have I left something out?" Martin asked.

"You might mention that it is said of the Americans that there is one standing on every square foot of English soil—and on Sunday mornings, not too steadily."

Martin laughed appreciatively at the anti-American joke.

"Well," Allison said, "I must say I admire your sense of humor."

"Thank you," Martin said. "Now, it's your turn."

"My turn?"

"Yes. Why would any American harbor a prejudice against the English?"

Allison thought for a moment. "That's hard to say," she said. "But perhaps you resent our self-righteous attitude about standing alone in the war for so long. I suppose we also have a rather superior air about us, a kind of one-upmanship which we British love to play."

"You are doing fine," Martin said. "Go on, don't stop now."

"The Americans have done a great deal for us," Allison said. "I suppose, in our haughty pride, we sometimes tend to be rather ungrateful."

"There now," Martin said. "Isn't confession good for the soul? Don't you feel better now?"

Allison laughed.

"It's good to see that you also have a sense of humor," Martin said. "Now, will you let me take you to breakfast?"

"All right," Allison said. "I suppose if you can overcome your prejudices, I can make a concerted effort to overcome mine. I would prefer it if you would dress before we go, however. While I may be induced to speak to, and even shake hands with a naked stranger, I refuse to eat breakfast with one."

"Right," Martin said, and he started to put on his clothes. The big smile never left his face as he dressed. When he slipped his jacket on, Allison saw the silver wings over his breast pocket.

"You are a pilot?"

"Yes," Martin said. "That was what I meant, earlier, when I said that without a navigator in the plane, I would never to able to find anything."

"My brother-in-law is a pilot," Allison said. "He flies Lancasters."

"Well, your brother-in-law and I are two peas in a pod," Martin said. "We both fly the heavies. I'm in B-17's."

Martin and Allison continued their conversation during breakfast. Allison laughed as Martin explained some of the adjustments he had had to go through.

"The post number for my mail is Z-109," Martin said. "I had a devil of a time trying to figure out what 'zed' was, until I realized that the English say 'zed' when they mean zee.''

"No," Allison laughed. "You Americans say 'zee,' when you mean *zed*."

"Who is to say who is right?" Martin asked.

"Whose language is it in the first place?" Allison replied. "After all, it is called 'English,' is it not? You Americans have merely borrowed it."

"Did you hear yourself just then?" Martin asked.

"What?" Suddenly Allison laughed and put her hand to her mouth. "The superiority thing, oh my, I just did it, didn't I?"

"That's all right, I've overcome that particular prejudice," Martin said, holding his hand up. "In fact, I'm proud to learn proper deportment from my betters." He laughed, and Allison laughed with him.

"What time do you have to be back to Wimbleshoe?" she asked.

Martin's eyes wrinkled in surprise. "How did you know I was stationed at Wimbleshoe?"

"I recognized your flash," Allison said. "I'm a driver, I've seen them before."

"My flash?"

"Oh, you Yanks call it a patch. A shoulder patch, I believe."

"Ah yes, my flash," Martin said. "The fearsome, facile, fighting Six Hundred and Fifth. Well, since my unit has been compromised, I may as well tell you everything. I'm due back tonight. I'll catch a flight out around seventeen hundred. Why do you ask?''

''I don't have to go to work until seventeen hundred myself. I thought perhaps you might be interested in a little picnic. We could—''

''Are you *serious*?'' Martin asked, interrupting her.

''Yes,'' Allison said. ''Of course, if you would rather not, I understand, and—''

''Listen, what are you talking about? I'd love to go on a picnic! In fact, I can't think of anything in the world I would rather do today than go on a picnic. Where will we go? Wait, we have to buy some stuff, don't we?''

Allison laughed at Martin's enthusiasm. ''We can take a train to a spot just out of the city. I know a place which is quite lovely for picnicking. There's a little village where the train stops—we could rent a couple of bicycles there, buy a few things from the grocer, then pedal out into the country. That is, if you agree.''

''It sounds wonderful,'' Martin said. ''In fact, it is the most wonderful-sounding thing I have heard since I arrived in this country.''

''Well then, shall we go?''

Martin hopped up quickly and came around to pull Allison's chair out for her as she stood. She looked around the restaurant and saw that several of the patrons were watching them. Some of the English citizens were barely able to conceal their contempt as they witnessed what they no doubt considered yet another of their girls succumbing to the charm of the American 'invaders.'

Allison experienced a moment of embarrassment, and she felt her face flush. Then, suddenly, she felt a sense of shame over her embarrassment. After all, Martin Holt had proven to be a remarkably pleasant young man, and she had no right to feel any embarrassment because of him. The others were just prejudiced, and they would have to live with their prejudices.

My word, Allison thought. Imagine such a thought coming from me. Until an hour ago, I would have willingly accepted the title of most prejudiced girl in all of England. She smiled at the thought.

"Why are you smiling?" Martin asked.

"I've just seen myself," Allison said. "And I never realized until now what a ludicrous figure I was."

"I don't understand."

"It doesn't matter," Allison said. "Come, or we shall miss the train."

Martin took the counter check over to pay for their breakfast. As he stood there, waiting for change to be made, he looked around at the others in the restaurant. He saw the looks on the faces of the others, and he realized that they were visibly disapproving of the relationship which seemed to be developing between an English girl and an American soldier. Then he understood what Allison had meant by her remark a moment earlier. He smiled and nodded his head toward them.

"Don't mind these people," he said to Allison, as they walked out of the place. "We who have overcome our prejudices have a difficult time understanding how anyone could be so ludicrous as to harbor ideas based upon ignorance."

"Yes, it is difficult to comprehend," Allison said.

"Aren't we the superior ones, though?"

"Quite," Allison agreed.

3

Victoria Station was crowded with wartime passengers and the noisy excitement of people going places. Allison bought their tickets, and they started toward their train. Just before their gate, they passed a vendor selling Coca-Cola from a stack of cases piled up behind him.

"Wait," Martin called, pulling on Allison to hold her back. "I'm dying for a Coke."

"Yes," Allison teased. "I've been told that Americans can't go more than twelve hours without one. It's a little like dope addiction, isn't it? You require a 'fix'?"

"Careful now, your prejudice is showing," Martin warned. He stepped up to the vendor. "Haven't you any cold ones?" he asked.

"Just took these out of the fridge, guv'," the vendor answered, popping the cap off a bottle and handing it to Martin. The Coke bubbled up from the bottle and spilled down over the sides, obviously warm.

Martin paid, took a swallow, and made a face. "Ugh," he said. "It's warm. But then, I don't know why I expected it to be cold. You drink everything else warm—even your beer."

"It does make it easier to handle things though, doesn't it?" Allison asked. "Aren't you glad we shan't have to lug ice along with us when we go out to our picnic?"

"You're right about that, I have to admit," Martin said.

They hurried through the gate and out onto the platform toward their train. There were several trains standing under the huge trainshed canopy, and the shed was a cacaphony of sound—here, a shrill whistle; there, a hiss of steam. Steam, like lace tendrils, floated up toward the high roof. Steel-rimmed carts rolled up and down the platforms, while baggage handlers and conductors shouted back and forth.

Allison pointed to the car they were to board. They got on and entered a small compartment right through the door. Though they found a seat, they were pushed close together by the press of the crowd.

A rather portly gentleman chose a seat right beside Martin, and Martin had to move so close to Allison that she could feel the heat of his leg as it pressed against hers. For some reason the heat seemed more intense than normal, and, transferred to her, it ran through her entire body. She thought of the scene in her bedroom earlier, and she recalled his near naked condition. That thought made her flush even more, and she felt a strange feeling in the pit of her stomach and a quickening of breath.

The train jerked and rattled as it began to move, and Allison watched the platform begin to slide by, slowly at first, and then more quickly, until finally the train raced free of the platform and the station area and headed out into the countryside.

"You're a Yank, aren't you?" a man dressed in civilian clothing said to Martin.

"Yes, sir, I am," Martin replied.

"Why don't you bloody Yanks leave our girls alone?" the man asked indignantly. He was in his mid-fifties, with white hair and blue eyes which flashed angrily as he made his denunciation.

"I beg your pardon?" Martin replied, surprised by the animosity in the man's voice.

The man took a pipe from his jacket pocket and pointed it at Martin, holding the bowl like a pistol grip and using the stem as its barrel.

"I asked why you don't leave our young girls alone," the man repeated. "After all, our young men are down in Africa, and Italy, fighting the

63

bloody war for you. They aren't in America now, are they? I mean, our lads aren't making time with your girls, while you are over here, so why the blazes are you making cuckolds of all our young men? And you, young lady, should be ashamed of yourself."

"I quite agree," Martin said easily, before Allison could respond. "The behavior of some of my countrymen has been abominable. But you misunderstand the relationship I have with this young lady. You see, she is my first cousin. Her mother is my mother's sister, and the family asked that I visit."

"Tell me, cousin," Allison said, playing along with Martin. "Did Maggie get the last letter I sent her? I did so want to thank her for the mittens she sent us in her 'bundles for Britain' package."

"Yes, Mother did receive the letter," Martin said, with a wink and a grin at Allison. "And she was so pleased with Aunt Millicent's reaction."

"Urmph, humph," the Englishman said, clearing his throat loudly. "Look here, old man, it would seem as if I am left sitting here with egg on my face. I'm really quite sorry if I spoke out of turn. I do hope you will forgive me. Of course, your being family and all, I quite understand. It's just that I have seen so many of you blokes with our girls, and I understand you Americans can be quite engaging, what with your frontierism, the wild west and all that. It all seems a shame, somehow."

"You needn't worry about a thing," Martin said. "If it weren't for strict orders from my mother to look up cousin Allison, I would be in some pub right now, drinking a glass of warm ale and enjoying a game of darts with my friends."

"Easy," Allison whispered, barely able to contain her giggles. "Don't go overboard now."

The two 'cousins' laughed and talked with each other for the next hour. Then, when the conductor walked through the car calling something which sounded like 'Medined,' Allison indicated that this was their stop.

The train station here was hardly different from the one at Wimbleshoe, a small brick station which was the center of activity for the village. When they stepped down from the train, an unexpected whoosh of steam escaped from one of the lines beneath the car, and Allison, startled, fairly jumped into Martin's arms. He put his arms around her.

"Oh," she said, looking up at him. "I'm sorry."

Martin looked into her face, and smiling broadly, made no effort to let her go. "Oh, don't be sorry," he said. "If I thought this might happen more often, I'd be willing to spend the rest of the day right here on the station platform."

Allison stood there wrapped in his arms, as if mesmerized by the moment, and made no effort to pull away until the train gave a shrill whistle. The whistle and the rattling movement of the train seemed to bring her back to a sense of reality, and she gently disengaged herself from Martin's embrace.

"We'll have to wait on this side until the train is gone," Allison explained. "The bicycle rental shop is across the track."

They stood there as the train moved by, car following car, each compartment full of men and women, both in uniform and out, everyone travelling with an air of importance which was exaggerated by the wartime conditions. When the last car finally clacked by, Allison led Martin across the track.

Suddenly, and inexplicably, Martin started to laugh.

"What is it?" Allison asked, surprised by his strange outburst.

"That," Martin said, pointing to a sign and laughing. "I didn't understand what the conductor was saying, but now I see. The name of this place is Maidenhead."

"Yes, our British names are sometimes quite colorful," Allison said. Then, suddenly realizing the significance of the name, she blushed.

"I'm sorry," Martin said gently. "It was indelicate of me to call attention to it. This village has probably had this name for a hundred years or more, and no one has found the occasion to make a dirty joke of it before. Will you forgive me?"

Martin's reaction surprised Allison. She had expected him to continue with his ribald humor, but instead he crossed her up with a streak of genuine tenderness and concern for her feelings. She was strangely moved by that.

"I'll forgive you, if you promise you won't say anything to your Aunt Millicent," Allison said with a smile.

"You have my word," Martin agreed.

"Millicent?" Allison said. "Where on earth did you come up with the name, Millicent?"

"Isn't that your mother's name?" Martin asked.

"No," Allison laughed. "Her name is Anne."

"Is that spelled with an 'e'?"

"Yes, A-n-n-e."

"Of course it would be spelled with an 'e'," Martin said. "Anyone who can't spell the word shop, without putting an extra 'p' and an 'e' on the end of it, certainly couldn't be expected to spell the name Ann without an 'e' after it. But, to answer your question about where I came up with the name Millicent, I was just looking for the most English name I could think of, and Millicent was the name."

Allison laughed. "I was just trying to come up with the most *American* name I could think of, and it was Maggie. I take it your mother's name isn't Maggie?"

"No," Martin said. "My mother's name is Nancy."

"Nancy? I suppose that is American enough. I might have preferred something more typical for an aunt, though."

"How about Dottie?"

"Dottie? Yes, yes, that's great."

"Well, that's the name of your cousin, my sister," Martin said. "Her real name is Dorothy, but we all call her Dottie."

"As I recall, Dorothy is the name of the little girl from Kansas in *The Wizard of Oz*," Allison said. "Oh, here is the place for the bicycles. Shall we go in?"

"Look at the sign," Martin said, pointing to the neatly painted sign over the front window. "S-h-o-p-p-e. Just like I said."

They pushed the door open and a small bell tinkled as they walked in. There was a whistling noise from the back of the building, obviously the sound of water being boiled. The whistling was interrupted as the kettle was taken from the heat.

"I'll be with you in just a jif," a man's voice called. "I'm taking a spot of tea."

"Oh, that sounds delightful, Mr. Tedder. You go right ahead and enjoy it. We'll just look around for a bit," Allison called back.

The curtain which hung in the door was parted, and a small baldheaded man peered through. His face broke into a big smile when he saw Allison.

"Lady Allison, it is so nice to see you again. How is your mother? I've been following her in the papers. We are awfully proud of her here."

"Mother is fine," Allison said. "I visited with my parents yesterday."

"And the Earl?"

"They are both fine," Allison said.

"I'm sorry I was so rude about the tea," Mr. Tedder said. "If the folks here knew I had treated Lady Anne's daughter so shabbily, they would rise up in arms. It's just that I've brought the water to boil twice before, and something has come up each time," he explained.

"Please," Allison said. "Do enjoy your tea. We are in no hurry."

"Won't you have a spot with me?"

"Thank you, no," Allison said. "We'll just look around for a bicycle to rent."

"You are most gracious, Lady Allison," Tedder said, and he stepped back behind the door curtain.

Martin had been shocked when he heard Tedder call Allison 'Lady Allison,' and the more Tedder talked, the more shocked he had become. Finally, he gave voice to his surprise.

"What did he call you?" Martin asked. "Did he say *Lady* Allison?"

"He's a bit of a traditionalist, I'm afraid," Allison said. She put her hand on one of the bicycles. "This one looks nice, don't you think? It has a wicker basket, which we shall need if we are to carry a picnic lunch with us."

"What does that mean?" Martin asked.

"Nothing, really," Allison said. "Now, let's find one for you." She was clearly trying to steer the conversation in other directions.

"Are you a lady?" Martin asked. He was just as clearly not going to give up.

"Well, I do like to think I'm a lady," Allison said. "After all, don't you consider yourself a gentleman?"

"You know what I mean," Martin said. "I mean are you a lady by title?"

"I suppose I am," Allison said. "But please, Martin, don't make such a big thing of it. You are a gentleman by title. Isn't that what they say of American officers? They are gentlemen, aren't they, by act of Congress?"

Tedder came in from the back of the shop, carrying a steaming cup. He put it on the counter, then grinned at the two young people.

"Ah, a bit of tea, and I'm my jolly old self right enough. Now, what can I do for you?"

"We want to rent a couple of bicycles," Allison said.

"Going for a bit of a ride, are you?"

"Yes," Allison said. "We're going on a picnic."

"Well, you've a nice enough day for it all right. Not like yesterday, with all that rain. Did it rain in London?"

"I don't know," Allison said. "I was at Ingersall yesterday, and we had very nice weather."

"I was in London, and it rained," Martin said.

"You're an American, aren't you?"

"Yes," Martin answered, immediately defensive.

"I know I'm not the first to welcome you, but I

do want all of you Americans to know how much we appreciate your getting into this war. Thank you, lad. Thank you very much.''

"I, uh, am glad to be here," Martin said, because he could think of nothing else to say.

Martin and Allison selected the bicycles, then left the shop and pedaled to the grocer for their lunch.

"What do you think?" Allison asked. "A little sausage?"

"Sausage?"

"Oh dear, I think I read once that the only sausage Americans know is the kind they cook for breakfast. When I say sausage, I'm really talking about a type of lunch meat. Like this, see?" She pointed to a cut of meat.

"Bologna," Martin said. "Or at least, something a little like bologna."

Allison laughed. "What was it George Bernard Shaw said? The British and the Americans are two great peoples, separated by a common language?"

Martin laughed at the comment, then pointed to a bottle of wine. "I didn't think there was any wine left in all of England. This bottle is for sale, isn't it?" he asked the grocer. "It isn't just to remind us of the fact that there is still wine, I hope."

"Indeed it is for sale," the grocer said. "I was fortunate enough to receive some California wine this month."

"California wine? I come all the way to Europe for California wine?"

"French and Italian wines, to say nothing of German wines, are a little difficult to come by just now," Allison said. "What don't you like about California wines? I thought they were supposed to be quite good."

"They are," Martin said. "They are excellent, in fact. I was just making a comment on the irony of it, that's all. We'll take this wine."

"We'll need a little cheese," Allison said. "And, of course, a loaf of bread."

"Oh, and a pickle," Martin said. "Do you have any pickles?"

The grocer smiled. "The war's caused many shortages, but we've plenty of pickles. A whole barrel, in fact. Just pick out what you want."

When Martin and Allison left the grocer, they had the basket of Martin's bicycle filled with food.

"Now where?"

"Follow me," Allison said, and she started on ahead.

Allison had ridden up this lane many times, not only on a bicycle, but on horseback as well. She didn't tell Martin, but the field in which they were going to picnic was owned by her mother's family. As a result, she was quite at home here.

It was a lovely sunny day. As they cycled down the lane, their wheels raised little rooster tails of dust that settled back on the bright yellow marigolds blooming on either side.

Allison stopped by a white gate, then opened it and motioned Martin through. Once he was through, she passed inside, then closed the gate behind them.

"Are you sure this is all right?" Martin asked a little nervously. "I don't want some angry farmer to come after us with a shotgun."

"It's all right," Allison assured him. She was amused by his nervousness.

They rode across a field of clover, then stopped by a gnarled old tree. Allison lay her bicycle over and began removing the groceries from Martin's basket.

"Listen," Martin said. "What is that?"

Allison laughed. "The great American outdoorsman has never heard a babbling brook before?"

Martin hurried to the top of a small hill and looked over the other side. He let out a whoop of joy. "It *is*," he said. "I was beginning to think no such thing existed in England. Have you ever heard anything so pretty? Listen to it."

"Well, I'm glad you approve of my picnic site," Allison said. "Bring the cloth, we'll spread it on the ground."

"I hope we have ants," Martin said.

"Ants?" Allison replied in surprise. "Did you say you hope we have ants?"

"Sure," Martin grinned. "A picnic's not a picnic without ants. Didn't you know that?"

Allison laughed as she put the food out, and laughed again as she pointed to a tiny red insect which was crawling across the cloth almost as quickly as she could spread it. "It looks as if you'll have your wish," she said.

Allison was about to kill the ant when Martin stopped her. "Don't do that," he said. "He's the recon. If you kill him, the others will never find out. Let him get back to make his report."

"Very well, if you insist," Allison said.

Martin took off his jacket and hung it from a tree branch. When he sat down, Allison saw him wince just a little as he put pressure on his knee.

"Does it hurt much?" she asked.

"What?"

"The flak wound," Allison said.

For a moment Martin looked puzzled, then he smiled. "You mean the knee? No, it's all right."

Allison put her hand on it. "It feels so mis-shapen," she said. "It must have hurt terribly when you were first wounded."

"It did," Martin said. He took the bottle of wine and began uncorking it, while Allison un-wrapped the cheese and sausage.

"Oh dear, I knew we would forget something," she said. "We don't have anything to cut the cheese and sausage with."

"Here," Martin said, handing her his pocket knife.

Allison opened the knife, and after cutting the

meat and cheese, she cut off some bread. Martin poured the wine in the paper cups they had remembered to bring from the grocer.

"Earl of what?" Martin asked.

"I beg your pardon?"

"The man in the bicycle shop asked about your mother and the earl. Your mother, I take it, is Lady Anne. If your father is an earl, isn't he the earl of something? Isn't that the way it works?"

"He is the Earl of Dunleigh," Allison said.

"And your mother is the Countess of Dunleigh?"

"Yes," Allison said. "But she is also the Countess of Warbo, in her own right."

"My god!" Martin gasped. "She almost married the King!"

"How on earth did you know that?" Allison asked, quite surprised by Martin's comment.

"You must remember what a sensation it was in America, when Edward abdicated his Crown to marry Mrs. Simpson?" Martin said.

"Yes, how well I remember," Allison said. "We were quite embarrassed by all the hoopla in America. But what does that have to do with my mother?"

Martin laughed. "My father runs a small newspaper. In his own way, he helped contribute to all the hoopla. We ran a series of articles on the royal family, and I remember in particular a story about the woman who, but for fate, would have been queen. Lady Anne Townsend, who inherited the

Warbo estate, was a frequent companion of Prince George. Something happened to the romance. He married another and then became king. It was a wonderful story of the twists of fate.''

''What happened to their romance was that there never really was the romance the papers tried to invent. The real romance happened later, when my father began courting my mother. And lucky for me it did happen, or I wouldn't be here.''

''And so here we both are,'' Martin said. ''I feel honored to be in such an august presence.''

''Are you making fun of me?'' Allison asked, with just a touch of hurt in her voice.

''No,'' Martin said quickly. He saw that Allison wasn't responding to his joke, and he put his hand out to touch hers. ''Listen, don't pay any attention to me. It's just that all this title business, well, it really is rather disconcerting to an American. We don't have them, you know.''

''I know, and I think therein lies your fascination with them. I've never known people to set such store by things as you Americans do our titles. They really mean nothing, except that my grandparents and their grandparents for many generations before them happened to own land. There is so little land in England that when someone does own a farm, they are titled. It's an accident of birth, like your being born an American, that's all.''

''You're right,'' Martin said. ''I should look at

76

it that way. After all, you certainly don't *seem* like a lady.''

"What?''

"I mean a *titled* lady,'' Martin quickly corrected.

"What do you think a titled lady is supposed to be like?''

"Well, I don't know exactly,'' Martin said. He laughed. "Older, I guess, with gray hair and lots of jewels. Oh, and a big bosom.''

"You mean my bosom isn't big enough?'' Allison asked, teasing Martin.

"Oh, no,'' Martin said quickly. "You've got a fine bosom, really—I mean . . .'' suddenly Martin realized that Allison was teasing him and he stopped in mid-sentence. "In fact,'' he said quietly. "I would even go so far as to say that I love your bosom, and your legs, and your thighs and—''

"Please,'' Allison said quickly, now fearing that it wouldn't take too much for the conversation to get entirely out of hand. "You've made your point.''

Suddenly an avalanche of sound beat down on them, and they looked up quickly to see a lone B-17, flying low, with two of the four propellers standing still. The engines were roaring, and one of them was making loud banging noises. The airplane was so low that they could see all the battle damage, every hole in the wings and fuselage.

"Oh, Martin!'' Allison gasped, putting her hand to her mouth. "Will he make it?''

"He has no fires,'' Martin said. "The controls

seemed to be working. If either one of the pilots are flying, it should make it.''

"I don't understand," Allison said. "If a pilot isn't flying, who would be?''

"If they were both dead, one of the crew would have to take over," Martin said.

Suddenly Allison realized that Martin had to face that same possibility every time he flew, and she shivered, as if she were very cold. Martin saw her shiver, and he put his arms around her and pulled her to him. His move caught Allison by surprise, but she welcomed it. As his arms wrapped around her, she leaned into him. Willingly, even eagerly, she offered her lips up to him.

Martin's first kiss was amazingly gentle, a gentle touch of his lips against hers. Her lips quivered under his, and his kiss deepened, though not as far as her urgency demanded, or his.

Finally, Martin broke off the kiss, then looked at Allison with a strange expression on his face.

"I'm sorry," he said.

"You're sorry?" Allison laughed softly. "Martin, don't you know I wanted to do that as much as you did? Couldn't you tell?''

"I had no right," Martin said.

"Why? Martin, don't tell me you are put off by all this business of a title? I told you, that title means nothing. Absolutely nothing.''

"No, it isn't that," Martin said.

"Well, then, what is it?''

78

Martin looked at Allison, and from the pain in his face and the agony mirrored deep in his eyes, she knew even before he said it.

"You . . . You're married, aren't you?" she asked, scarcely daring to even speak the words.

"Yes," Martin said. "Forgive me, Allison, I should have told you."

Allison let out an audible sigh. "Yes," she finally said, speaking quietly. "Yes, you should have."

"I'm sorry," Martin said again.

"Listen, perhaps we had better hurry our lunch and start back," Allison suggested. "After all, I do have to work this evening."

"Yes," Martin said. "And I have to catch a flight back to Wimbleshoe. I suppose you're right."

They finished the meal quickly, and though their conversation went on, for Allison, it was a conversation which was strained by two, indisputable facts. Fact number one was that Martin Holt was married. Fact number two was that, despite all reason and logic, Allison was in love with him.

4

Lady Anne Townsend Cairns-Whiteacre, by marriage, Countess of Dunleigh and by inheritance Countess of Warbo, was, by the very nature of her life, not an inconspicuous person. She had once been linked romantically with Prince George. Given the unexpected abdication of George's older brother Edward, George ultimately became King of England. Had the romance progressed, Lady Anne might have become his Queen.

Lady Anne had been much in the news during the time of her romance with Prince George. Later, during the abdication, she had been thrust back into the news with the international glut of gossip concerning everyone who had ever had anything to do with the royal family. As she was also a very popular and much beloved personage in her own right, she couldn't even attend to the slightest public matter without attracting attention.

The British Home Defense utilized Lady Anne's high visibility to recruit volunteers for the British Ladies' Hospital Brigade. As its head, Lady Anne's movements were well publicized, and her pictures appeared in magazines, newspapers and newsreel films in England, Canada and the United States.

There was another reason that Lady Anne's comings and goings were so well publicized. Since she could not move about inconspicuously, it was decided that her movements should be made as conspicuous as possible, in order to mask something else. Depending upon the axiom to 'hide in plain sight,' Lady Anne was hiding her most important activity.

Lady Anne was not only the head of the British Ladies' Hospital Brigade; she was also on the advisory board of the First Aid Nursing Yeomanry, better known as FANY. It would seem logical for the head of the British Ladies' Hospital Brigade to be associated with FANY, as the public purpose of both organizations was to provide nursing care for the wounded. But FANY had another, and highly secret, purpose. FANY was the vehicle for all female espionage agents. Women recruited for espionage work were inducted into FANY. They were given khaki uniforms to wear, and trained for their real work under the cover of being nurses.

Lady Anne had a remarkable talent for detail and an amazing memory for trivia. She had often amused and amazed her friends with stories of her travels through Europe, in which not even the most minor details were ever omitted.

Lady Anne had such excellent powers of observation that she was able to discern the most subtle variation in a person's speech or dress that would identify the area, the city or even the section of the city from which the person came. Percival knew this, and when he had learned that there was a desperate need for volunteers to work as 'conducting officers' for the British Secret Service, he had volunteered Lady Anne.

The job of the conducting officer was extremely critical to the British Secret Service. The COs were responsible for interviewing prospective candidates, supervising their training and certifying them for assignment to their posts in occupied Europe, where the agents would function as 'pianists.' 'Pianist' was the code word for radio operator.

Once the pianists were on station, the COs continued to work with them by monitoring their performance with a particular eye on their style and the content of their reports. They did this by a psychological evaluation of the messages the agents sent back. Were the agents still in place or were the messages now coming from Germans posing as agents? Were the messages being sent under the coercion of German pistols or were they genuine reports? At what point would the agents' psychological and mental limits be reached? When should the agents be withdrawn?

The secrecy surrounding the identity of the agents in place was no greater than the secrecy surrounding the identity of the COs. If the German agents in England were able to discover the identity of the COs, they might be able to uncover the location and identities of each agent within the COs' stable. Because of that, the COs were very jealous of their privacy, and it was rare that even immediate members of their family knew of their avocation. Lady Anne's husband knew about her role because he was a highly-placed general, and had, in fact, recruited her. But none of her daughters knew. Lady Anne went to great lengths to ensure that they never learned, for each of them was in contact with so many people that the chances of leaks would be greatly intensified if they did know.

One of the most difficult tasks for Lady Anne was interviewing prospective agents. It was difficult because the interview had to be conducted in such a subtle way that the person being interviewed could ever realize the real purpose of of the interview. That way, if the candidate proved to be unacceptable, there would be no compromise of the secrecy. That meant they had to be both subtle and conclusive.

The interviews were also difficult for another, a more personal reason. Once the candidates were selected and the training had begun, the agent became one of Lady Anne's girls; often, Lady Anne found herself growing close to them until they were almost like her own daughters.

When the pianist's training was completed, Lady Anne had to validate it. That was where her own peculiar talent came into play, for she had to scrutinize the girls to make certain there was nothing about them which would attract suspicion. Finally, she had to authorize their assignments to their posts. For many, this assignment was also a death warrant.

One girl, who worked under the code-name 'Carmen,' had made a particular impression on Lady Anne. She had first heard of the young girl a few months earlier, when she was given the assignment of interviewing her.

"Tell me about the girl I am to interview today," Lady Anne had asked Mark, her contact in the British Secret Service, when they met at the Hotel Victoria.

"Her name is Linda Starberg," Mark said. Mark wasn't his real name; he had never told Lady Anne his real name, and she had never asked.

"She was born here in London," Mark went on. "Her father was an American Jew and her mother was a circus performer . . . and that is the secret of her qualifications. She traveled with her mother and father all over Europe, and she has lived in Paris, Madrid, Nuremberg and Brussels. She speaks six languages fluently. Her mother was an aerialist, killed in a performance in Stockholm. Her father was so despondent over the accident that he committed suicide, and Linda has been on her own for the last ten years. She was only fourteen when the accident happened, and she gained a marvelous sense of independence as well as the ability to feel at home no matter where she is.''

''I must confess, her qualifications sound excellent,'' Lady Anne said.

''Yes,'' Mark agreed. ''There is, however, one thing which may be a problem.''

''And that is?''

''She is an exceptionally pretty girl,'' Mark said. ''She has a dark and sultry beauty, dark brown hair and eyes, an olive complexion—the kind of arresting beauty which is bound to attract attention no matter where she goes. I'm afraid Linda could never fade into the background.''

''Yes,'' Lady Anne said. ''That could be a problem. But perhaps it is a problem which could be handled.''

''On the other hand, maybe it won't be a problem at all,'' Mark suggested. ''Look at Mata Hari. Her beauty certainly didn't hinder her effectiveness.''

"No," Lady Anne agreed. "But it did get her shot."

"Yes," Mark said. "Yes, I guess you are right at that. I didn't think of that."

Lady Anne looked at the clock. "Oh dear, it is nearly time for the interview. I had better get on up to the room. I wouldn't want her to get there before I do."

"Good luck," Mark said.

Lady Anne and Mark had met in one of the meeting rooms of the Hotel Victoria on Northumberland Avenue, the site for all candidate interviews. The hotel rooms, staff and guests were kept under constant surveillance by the British Secret Service to ensure that it was always a 'safe' house. After her discussion with Mark, Lady Anne had but a short walk to the room where the interview would be conducted.

There was a mirror in the lobby of the hotel, and Linda checked her appearance before she went up for the interview. She had no idea whom she was to meet today or why, for that matter, she was going to meet her. A friend of hers had suggested strongly that this meeting might prove to be very useful to her.

Her friend had been very vague as to what usefulness the meeting would serve, but Linda's curiosity had been piqued, and she'd decided to keep the appointment.

Linda took the lift to the fifth floor, then walked down the carpeted hallway until she found room 505. She knocked lightly.

The door opened, and Linda found herself looking into the face of an attractive, vaguely familiar middle-aged woman. The woman was wearing a well-tailored uniform with a shoulder flash reading: *British Ladies' Hospital Brigade.*

What is this? Linda thought. Am I being recruited to work as a nurse?

"Linda, how good of you to keep the appointment. My name is Anne. Won't you come in?"

"Thank you," Linda said. She came in at the woman's invitation and took the seat Anne offered her.

"Would you like some tea?"

"Yes, thank you," Linda said. Linda watched as the tea was poured, then accepted the cup.

"Now," Anne said, "let's get down to business, shall we? Have you ever heard of the First Aid Nursing Yeomanry?"

"Yes," Linda said, "I believe I have."

"We have a mutual friend, Linda, who tells me you might be able to perform a valuable service for us."

Linda smiled. "I fear this friend may be a bit over-zealous in extolling my talents," she said. "I have no talent in nursing; indeed, I behave very badly when I'm around sick or injured people. I have a feeling of helplessness which frustrates me and I become quite useless.''

''Would you be interested in helping in some capacity other than nursing?'' Anne asked.

''What else is there in a nursing corps besides nursing?'' Linda asked.

''Oh, there are many areas in which you might be useful, if you were so inclined,'' Anne said. ''When a country is at war, it must call on all its citizens, women as well as men. Women have traditionally provided nursing, of course, and we of the FANY organization and the British Ladies' Hospital Brigade are very proud of our contribution in that capacity. But one must also consider such things as communication, interpretation . . . I'm told you speak more than one language.''

''I speak English, French, German, Spanish, Italian and Polish,'' Linda said.

''Of course, English is your native language,'' Anne said. ''But which languages are easiest for you?''

Linda laughed. ''I feel equally at home with all of them. I don't consider English any more native than French or German. I am a citizen of the world.''

''Yes, but you hold a British passport,'' Anne reminded her. ''And you are in England now. How do you feel, politically, about the belligerents in the war?''

''My father was Jewish,'' Linda said. ''That is

a distinction one cannot help but consider when viewing this war. I want Hitler and his gang of thugs removed from power. I want their reign of terror ended in Europe. I told you that I am a citizen of the world, but that world has now been closed to me. It is a little like living in a big house and being restricted to one room.''

"That's very well put, Linda,'' Anne said. "Now, excuse me, dear . . . This may sound like a rather foolish request, but believe me, it is very important. Without looking around, could you describe this room for me?''

"Yes,'' Linda said easily. She closed her eyes. "To the left of the door there is a chair, Queen Anne in style and white with light blue upholstery. Beside it is a white table, and on the table a white lamp trimmed in gold. The lamp has no lightbulb. On the wall to the left is a sofa, also white and blue, and above the sofa there is a large painting. It's a pastoral scene with a stream and yellow flowers. It really isn't a very good painting; the perspective is bad. The sofa is flanked by end tables and lamps; the lamp to the left of the sofa is burning, but the other is not. The carpet is dark blue and does not extend all the way to the wall. On the wall opposite the sofa is a picture of King George, and . . .'' Suddenly Linda smiled broadly and opened her eyes to look in Anne's face. "Now I know,'' she said. "You are Lady Anne Cairns-Whiteacre.''

"George gave me away, did he?" Lady Anne asked. She smiled. "You have a remarkable talent for observation and detail, Linda. You would be excellent for our purposes, should you decide to work with us. Tell me, of all the places you have lived, which do you like the best?"

Linda smiled. "Paris," she said.

"Do you know Paris very well?"

"I know Paris better than I know London," Linda said. "I would still be there, if it weren't for the fact that any place occupied by the Nazis is unsafe for Jews."

"What if I told you I could arrange it for you to go back to Paris with a new identity?" Lady Anne asked. "Passports, papers, everything you would need to pass yourself off as a French citizen."

"You could do that?"

"Yes, quite easily."

"This is what this is all about, isn't it?" Linda asked. "You want me to go back to Paris, don't you?"

"Only if you want to go," Lady Anne said. "But I must warn you, the job we would want you to do is dangerous. It is so dangerous that there is a very real possibility you could be killed."

"That's something to think about, isn't it?" Linda replied. "Would this job, whatever it is, really be worth the risk?"

"Yes. It would make a very positive contribution toward ending Hitler's reign of terror," Lady

Anne said. "But tell me, Linda—am I frightening you?"

"Yes, I have to admit you are," Linda said.

"Good," Lady Anne replied with a smile. "If you weren't frightened, we wouldn't be interested in you. Now, the big question, Linda: are you interested in us?"

"Yes," Linda said.

Lady Anne looked at the beautiful girl across the table from her. She had passed every facet of the interview. There was no reason why she shouldn't be accepted. And yet it was a sad thing too, for by accepting this delightful young girl, Anne was placing her in a situation where she could face unspeakable horror. Lady Anne sighed.

"I am empowered to offer you a position as a radio operator in one of our underground networks in Paris," she said. "If you accept it, you will be trained and then sent to Paris, where you will maintain radio contact with us while working as a liaison between the Free French Underground and the British Secret Service. If you do not wish to accept, get up and walk away now, and you will never be contacted again."

"And if I do wish to accept?" Linda asked.

Lady Anne closed her eyes for a moment, then opened them and looked into the eager, trusting face.

"Your code name will be Carmen," she said.

*   *   *

Linda's training began immediately after her recruitment. A ration book and identity papers were prepared for her, declaring her to be Algerian with the name of Kani Ben-Ahr. She was given a wardrobe consistent with the clothes worn in the part of Algeria which her identity papers specified. The wardrobe was accurate down to the last detail, down to every stitch in the wartime cloth. She was furnished with pills, knockout pills she could use on others and pep-up pills for herself, as well as a pill which would cause her own immediate death, should it ever become necessary.

Linda learned how to disable a would-be assailant with a well-placed knee or a chop of the hand. She discovered how common everyday objects could be turned into lethal weapons. She learned how to shoot a pistol and bail out of an aircraft at night. But, most important of all, she learned how to operate the radio.

There was more to operating the radio than merely learning Morse Code. She had to learn the Morse Code and then a code within a code, for the transmissions had to be brief as actual word messages were never sent. So it was that certain letter groups took on the meaning of certain phrases, and Linda had to master each of them. The one she learned first was 'QUO,' which meant she was in immediate danger and could not transmit.

Linda's training lasted for three months. She

saw Lady Anne many times during those three months, but always under the pretext of some business pertaining to nursing, such as the capping of actual nursing graduates or the organization of a new volunteer nursing unit. During those times, which were filled with cameras and public announcements, Lady Anne always managed, somehow, to speak to Linda alone, and to discuss her training. Lady Anne was amazingly attuned to Linda's progress—and even to her personal life, as Linda discovered, to her shock, during one of their meetings.

"You spoke with Arthur this week, didn't you?" Lady Anne asked.

"You . . . you *know* about Arthur?"

"I know you had an affair with him," Lady Anne said. "And I know that he wouldn't divorce his wife. I thought—that is, I hoped—that it was all over."

"It is," Linda said.

"Believe me, Linda, I'm not passing judgment on your affair with a married man. But you cannot afford any complications in your life right now, and Arthur Brisbane is a complication."

"I know," Linda said contritely. "I don't know why I went to see him again. I just felt that I had to see him one more time. I thought if I saw him again, I would realize how much better off I was without him. But don't worry. We said very little to each other, and I said nothing of consequence."

"I know you didn't," Lady Anne said. "In fact, I know everything each of you said."

"What? How could you possibly know all that?"

"From the moment you were accepted into this program, you have been under constant observation," Lady Anne said.

"I . . . I had no idea."

"I know you didn't, and that is what frightens me," Lady Anne said. "Linda, I have to authorize your assignment. If you were able to fall prey to our surveillance so easily, what do you think will happen when you come up against the Nazis? Believe me, their methods are much more effective— and deadly."

"I'll be more careful in the future."

"You've put me in quite a spot, Linda," Lady Anne said.

"What are you saying?" Linda asked. "Are you implying that I may not get to go to France? Are you saying you won't recommend me?"

"I don't know if I should," Lady Anne said.

"Please, you must," Linda begged. "I know I can do this job. I know I can."

"Let me think about it," Lady Anne said as she left.

Linda had studied the Morse Code so diligently that she literally dreamed it. And in her dream she was in a room with several other people, none of whom could speak. They all had to communicate by sending coded messages.

Suddenly a blinding flash of light interrupted Linda's dream, and she heard a loud sound as her door was slammed.

"Get up! Get up, you sow!" a rough, guttural voice commanded. He was speaking in German, but as Linda was fluent in German, it didn't register for a moment that she was being ordered about in a foreign language. Then, as she became fully awake, she realized that her room had been invaded by a squad of German SS men.

"What are you doing here?" Linda demanded.

"Shut up, sow! We will ask all the questions," the SS Captain said. He nodded his head, and the others grabbed her, then bound and gagged her. She struggled against them, but it was no use. She was blindfolded and taken from her room. A moment later she was thrown into the back of a car. After a hard drive of nearly an hour, she was pulled out of the car and dragged roughly into a building. When the blindfold was removed, she saw that she was in some kind of dungeon. Her captors pushed her into an empty cell and locked the door, then left her there.

"Wait!" she called after them. "Who are you? What is all this about?"

Linda saw no one for the remainder of the day. Twice, however, a small window opened, and a disembodied arm shoved through a tray containing one slice of bread and one cup of water. At one point she heard a terrifying scream, one so horrible in its pitch that she couldn't even tell if it was a man or a woman.

What had happened to her? How did the SS men get to London?

Much later, possibly as late as the next day, Linda was taken from her cell to an office, where an SS officer began shouting questions at her.

"Who is the head of your organization?"

"What organization?" Linda replied.

"How were you recruited?"

"I don't know what you are talking about."

"Who else is in this with you?"

Linda remained silent.

"Where were you going to be assigned?"

Linda refused to answer all the questions, even when one of the officers put a pistol to her head and pulled the trigger. When she heard the snap of an empty gun, she nearly fainted.

After that, another SS officer came into the room. He also spoke sharply, but not to Linda. He reprimanded the officer who had been interrogating her for mistreating the prisoner.

"I'm sorry, Fraulein Starberg," he said. "Ah yes, we do know your name. Your *real* name. But you have lived among the German people, and you know we are not the monsters the British have painted us to be. I'm asking you now, in the spirit of cooperation one might expect from a citizen of the world, won't you cooperate with us? We could quite easily put you in place as a double agent and pay you handsomely, and you could continue to be a citizen of the world. Wouldn't that be far preferable to the danger to which the British would have you exposed? What do you say, Fraulein? Won't you help us?''

"No," Linda said.

"Fraulein, if you do not help us, you will be killed! Are you too stupid to understand that?''

"I won't help you," Linda said, so frightened that she could barely mumble the words.

The officer sighed. "Perhaps I was wrong to interfere," he suggested. "Perhaps I should have let the others have their way with you, perhaps rape you—oh yes, they are bestial people—and then kill you. Is that what you want?''

"No," Linda said quietly.

"Then you *will* cooperate with us?''

"No," Linda said again.

The German officer sighed, then stepped back. "She is all yours," he said.

Linda hung her head, waiting for what might come next.

The door opened, and Lady Anne came into the room.

"I'm sorry, dear," she apologized. "This was the last and certainly the most difficult test of the entire course. You passed it."

"This—this was a test?" Linda asked in a small voice. She was shaking uncontrollably.

"Yes," Lady Anne said. "I'm sorry it was necessary to frighten you so. But I must caution you—this was nothing compared to a real Gestapo interrogation."

"But I did pass?" Linda asked. "That means I can go, doesn't it?"

"You will be on the plane tonight," Lady Anne said. "You'll be in Paris before morning."

5

"Air Chief Marshall Harris will see you now," the adjutant told General Sir Percival Cairns-Whiteacre.

"Thank you," Percival said. He laid aside the magazine he'd been reading, and walked into the office of the Chief of British Air Operations.

"Well, Sir Bomber," Percival said, smiling and extending his hand. "It's good to see you again."

The 'Sir Bomber' title was a joking reference to the fact that Air Chief Marshal Arthur Harris had been knighted shortly after the phenomenal 1,000-plane raid over Cologne, France, the year before.

"Percy, the pleasure is all mine," the Air Chief Marshal said. "Sit down, won't you?"

The General accepted the invitation and nodded when Harris pointed to the hot water kettle. The Air Chief Marshal began steeping two cups of tea.

"Do you take sugar?"

"Two lumps, please," Percival said.

"Percy, let me tell you why I asked you here. To get right to the point, I want you to help me with the bloody Americans."

"Help you? In what way, Arthur?"

Harris finished preparing the tea and handed Sir Percival a cup before taking a seat.

"They insist upon continuing with the daylight bombing," Harris said. "It's insane. Their losses are staggering—in fact, they may very well catch up with our own losses soon, and we have been at it for three years longer."

"Arthur, I quite agree with you. It is difficult to understand why the Americans would even wish to continue with such a policy in face of such losses. But it is their decision to make, isn't it?"

"Percy, one year ago, on the occasion of my picking up a little flourish for my name, I issued a statement to the press. Whenever anyone is knighted, the press seems to think they will have a pearl of wisdom to share with everyone else, and they always ask for a statement. Well, let me tell you, the statement I gave to the press *was* a pearl of wisdom. I said that victory would come to the

nty thousand feet. With it the Americans
achieve what they were calling "precision"
. Precision bombing, the Americans in-
ould systematically deprive the Germans of
ories, railroad marshalling yards, submarine
other such critical targets. The British, the
is said, only spread terror and death and
on among civilians with their saturation
techniques.

not without good reason that 'Sir Bomber'
id called upon Percival Cairns-Whiteacre to
th the Americans. He was rapidly becoming
sh General with whom the Americans dealt
d the one who enjoyed the best rapport
m. Harris was not the only one to realize
neral Morgan had also called upon Sir
s talent for dealing with the Americans.

al climbed into the back of the staff sedan.
laxed in the deep cushioned seat, he found
wishing he had a command in Africa.
ie would be assigned to combat duty, per-
h an Infantry division, and everyone would
te his contribution. It was easy to be a
commander. Your task was clearly laid out
ou: meet and defeat the enemy. Here, one
valk a tightrope in order to ascertain just
e's duty really was. It was easy enough to
ight thing, he thought. The difficulty was
ing what the right thing was.
, sir?" the driver asked.

country which best understood, and utilized, its
air-power. I meant that."

"I think it is a statement of some validity,"
Percival agreed.

"Then why in the blazes didn't Chruchill *listen*
to me?" Harris asked, slamming his hand down on
his desk so hard that his tea cup rattled in its
saucer. "Why has he let the Americans pull the
wool over his eyes with this daylight bombing
policy of theirs? Listen, if we could convince the
Americans to give that up and to merge their
planes with ours for the night raids, we could bring
this war to a close months earlier. Months, do you
understand? When the balloon finally does go up
and we do land our lads in Europe, Jerry will have
very little spirit left to oppose them. We'll have
bombed the Germans back into the Stone Age."

"Arthur, I understand what you are saying,"
Percival said. "I might even agree with you. But
what can I do? I have no authority in these matters.
I'm not even in the Air Force. I hold my King's
Guards' Commission in the Army Reserve."

"I know," Harris said. "But you *are* in charge
of every square inch of real estate the Americans
use. That means you have a unique position of
influence over them. Surely you can discuss the
daylight bombing with them, can't you?" Harris
leaned closer to Sir Percival. "Do you know what
it reminds me of? The bloody charge of the Light
Brigade. It's all very noble and all that, but they

are pissing away their aircraft and some damned fine men in this gesture of futility."

"Very well," Percival said. "I will talk to them. But—and I feel compelled to make this point, Arthur—I don't expect to have much success."

"Well, try, man. That's all I ask."

"What about Churchill? Shouldn't he be the one to plead our case?"

"I've been to the Prime Minister time and time again," Harris said. "He is totally obsessed with something General Eaker of the American Air Force told him. Eaker said that the American strategy of bombing by day, coupled with our strategy of bombing by night, would never allow the Germans a moment of rest. Can you imagine selling such a concept with a statement like that? But Churchill bought it, and now we have two totally different policies instead of one unified plan."

"I'll discuss the situation with the few Americans I know," Percival said. "But I'm afraid I can't promise anything."

Harris ran his hand through his hair, then laughed nervously. "Understand, Percy, it is just that I am so convinced that they should change the policy that I am trying every avenue open to me. I would even write letters to Franklin Delano Roosevelt if I thought I could avoid trouble from Number 10 Downing Street."

"Oh, no, I shouldn't think you would care to do anything like that," Percival said with a laugh.

"Don't think I haven't [...]
Harris said. "You will [...]
results, won't you?"

"Yes, of course." Si[...]
of his tea and set his [...]
saucer. "Arthur, regardl[...]
in convincing the Americ[...]
let me say that all Engla[...]
you and your brave lads [...]

"Thank you," Harris [...]
had an easy time of it. [...]
step of the way, although [...]
through to the dunderhea[...]
them that area saturation[...]
fire way to achieve resu[...]
must admit, however, th[...]
of bombing the hydroe[...]
region, and events subse[...]
I'm not afraid to admit [...]
one. I wish a few ot[...]
disposition."

Harris walked the Ge[...]
the two men shook hands[...]

As Percival walked to [...]
the meeting. He had agre[...]
cans about their dayligh[...]
knew it would do no go[...]
exceptionally proud of th[...]
sight, a device which w[...]
that it could "place a [...]

from tw[...]
hoped to [...]
bombing[...]
sisted, [...]
their fac[...]
pens an[...]
America[...]
destruct[...]
bombing[...]

It was[...]
Harris h[...]
speak w[...]
the Brit[...]
most a[...]
with the[...]
this; G[...]
Percival[...]

Perci[...]
As he r[...]
himself [...]
There, [...]
haps wi[...]
appreci[...]
combat [...]
before [...]
had to [...]
what o[...]
do the [...]
in know[...]
"Yes[...]

Percival looked at the girl's reflection in the mirror. She was a young, attractive blonde. He wondered if she knew Allison, and he almost asked, but he was afraid that it might embarrass Allison. After all, she was trying to function outside the realm of his influence.

She had even dropped the Whiteacre from her name and was known only as Allison Cairns.

"Where to, sir?" the driver asked again.

"Oh, I'm sorry," Percival answered easily. "I suppose I must have been thinking of something else. Take me to the American Air Force headquarters, please."

"Yes, sir," the girl said, and skillfully pulled the car into the traffic.

Percival chuckled. Ten years ago there were few British girls who could even drive a car. Now there were hundreds, just like this girl and Allison, who not only drove, but drove with an expertise unmatched by many men. Sir Percival Cairns-Whiteacre believed that women possessed a great reservoir of untapped strength. It was something he was careful never to underestimate.

The American Army Air Corps Headquarters was housed in a white building with a landscaped garden and a curving driveway. It had been a library, before it was turned over to the Americans for their use. On the ground, in front of the flagpole, was a large plaque featuring the 8th Air Corps insignia—a large white number 8 in a star, riding a comet's tail across a blue sky, with smaller stars all around it. It was quite garish, and totally unbecoming to the landscaping which had taken a century to develop, but as it did no permanent damage to the garden, no one could really justify complaining about it.

The young lady who was driving the car hurried around to open the door for Percival. She blushed slightly, as two passing soldiers whistled at her. They moved away quickly when they saw the General climb out of the car.

"I must say I approve of their taste, if not their manners," Percival said.

"Thank you, sir," the girl replied, obviously pleased by the General's remark.

Percival hurried up to the headquarters building. Returning the guard's salute, he stepped through the door and into the building itself.

General Eaker wasn't there, but Percival did manage to speak with Major General Curt Porter, his counterpart in the American Army. Porter was the one who designated the American requirements for airfields and supply dumps, while Percival had the duty of providing the space. The two men worked well together, and General Porter greeted Percival warmly.

"What can I do for you?" Porter asked. "Perhaps I could offer you some coffee?"

"Thank you, no," Percival said. "I just had tea . . . with Air Chief Marshal Harris, as a matter of fact."

Porter, who was pouring a cup of coffee for himself, looked up quickly.

"Air Chief Marshal Harris? Oh, oh—why do I feel like I'm about to be cold-cocked with a five-pound sledge?"

Percival chuckled. "I must say, you chaps do have a most colorful language. We must try to borrow it sometime. You know I would never hit you with a . . . what did you say? A five-pound sledge? Whatever that is."

"It's a big-assed hammer," General Porter explained.

"Now, Curt, would I use a hammer? A cricket bat perhaps, or maybe even a croquet mallet, but never a hammer."

"What's on Sir Bomber's mind, as if I didn't know?" Porter asked. "No, let me guess. He's still making a pitch to get us to give up daylight precision bombing."

"You guessed it," Percival said.

"He's fighting a losing battle, Percy," Porter said. "And to tell the truth, I'm a little surprised that you would side with him. I thought you were on our side."

"Well, actually, that's really the point, isn't it?" Percival replied. "I mean, aren't we all on the same side in this war? We are allies, after all, and I should think that, though there are bound to be disagreements among allies, those disagreements should be worked out quite amicably."

"I hope we can work this out amicably," Porter said. "Because to tell you the truth, I thought we already had this thing settled. I mean, hell, Churchill himself is behind us on this thing."

"You must admit, though, that you are losing rather a disproportionate number of planes and crews," Percival said. "And, I might add, they are planes and crews that you can ill afford to lose at this juncture."

"Come into the briefing room with me," Porter said, somewhat mysteriously. Percival followed him into an adjoining room, the walls of which were covered with maps and charts. It was empty right now, and Porter summoned a guard.

"Stand by the door, would you, Corporal?" he said to the guard. "I'm going to give General Whiteacre a classified briefing."

"Yes, General," the guard said. As he moved into position by the door, Porter pulled it shut, then walked over to Percival.

"I'll admit we've had some problems, Percy," he said. "But soon those problems will be solved. We are shortly to receive new fighter planes which will have the range to escort our bombers all the way to targets deep inside Germany. Not only that, but we've been promised an additional 944 bombers. Think of it! By God, Percy, 944 bombers will put us at parity with the British. This country is going to look like one huge aircraft carrier. Do you have any idea what that all means?"

110

"I would say it could mean trouble for the Germans," Percival said.

"You're damned right it does," Porter said. He walked over to one of the tables and pulled a cigar from a box. He offered it to Percival, but Percival declined. Porter lit it up with lusty puffing and a huge cloud of smoke.

"Curt, I need something to take back to Harris, something that will show him a degree of cooperation between the two Air Forces. Is there nothing you can give me?"

Porter puffed reflectively for several seconds, then took the cigar from his mouth and used it as a pointer for the map of Germany on the wall.

"I'll tell you one thing you can give him," he said. "Even as we are talking, the 605th Bombardment Group is bombing the hell out of Schweinfurt."

"Schweinfurt?" Percival said. "The ball bearings plant?"

"We're taking it out," Porter said. "After today, the damned krauts won't have enough bearings left to start a game of marbles. Did you know that eighty percent of all their bearings are produced in Schweinfurt? This will cripple 'em. Hell, it'll bring Germany to her knees!"

"When do you expect your strike report?" Percival asked.

"Soon," Porter said. He looked at his watch. "Damned soon. Come on—if you want, you can be there when the strike report comes in. Then, if you still want to, you can talk to the old man. I don't have the authority to give a sop to Harris, but he can. Maybe the two of you can work something out.''

"Thanks," Percival said. "I appreciate that."

Porter opened the door and the guard outside came to attention. The two generals walked down the hall and past another guard, into a room at the end. There were several more senior officers standing around and nervously drinking coffee and smoking cigarettes. A young, nervous-looking enlisted man wearing earphones sat at a table with his fingers poised over the keys of a typewriter.

"There's the old man," Porter said, and General Eaker nodded at Percival. Returning the nod, Percival sat in one of the chairs and watched the Americans as they paced back and forth.

Suddenly the enlisted man spoke aloud.

"General Eaker, the strike report is coming in, sir," he said.

The young man's fingers began flying across the keyboard of the typewriter, and a colonel stepped into position behind him to read the report as it was typed.

"Action report, 6-6-43-1," the Colonel read. "Reached primary at 1021 zebra, cloud cover 3/10ths. All planes bombed primary . . .''

"Yahoo!" one of the others shouted, and his shout was echoed by many of the others.

The young man at the typewriter didn't join in with the celebration, but continued to type.

"All planes bombed primary," the Colonel said again. "Estimated target destruction at 95%."

Again there was a spontaneous shout of celebration from the officers gathered.

"Flak exceptionally heavy, fighter aircraft exceptionally heavy, eighty-two . . ." The Colonel stopped reading and looked at the others. There was a dead silence, except for the continuing clack of the typewriter. The Colonel cleared his throat.

"Go on, Bud," General Porter said.

"Eighty-two aircraft lost enroute to target," the Colonel announced quietly. "Many more damaged."

"Eighty-two?" Porter said. "My God, Bud— did you say *eighty*-two?"

"Yes, sir," the Colonel said quietly.

The mood of celebration which had erupted a moment earlier quickly disappeared. The Colonel stopped reading the report, and though a few officers gathered behind the young man to read the remainder, most of them left the room. They walked out quietly.

Percival followed Porter out into the hallway, where Porter approached General Eaker.

"Percy would like to talk to you, General," Porter said.

"I can wait until later, General," Percival said quickly. "I understand that this is probably not the best time to talk."

"Come on into my office, Percy," General Eaker invited. "You too, Curt."

The two men followed him in, and General Eaker sat down behind his desk. He held his head in his hands for a moment, then sighed.

"You're right, Percy," he said. "This isn't a good time to talk. Eighty-two aircraft. That's eight hundred and twenty men, to say nothing of those killed or wounded on the other planes. But the war has to go on, so we'll talk. What's on your mind?"

"I just came from a visit with the Air Chief Marshal," Percival said. "He asked that I speak to you."

"You can guess what he wants," Porter put in.

"I know what he wants," Eaker said, leaning back in his seat. "He wants me to abandon daylight precision bombing. And after the results of this mission become generally known, I'm afraid he'll have some support from a few people on our side."

"General Arnold?" Porter asked. "Surely he wouldn't abandon us, would he?"

"No," Eaker said. "Hap is behind us one hundred percent. General Whiteacre, this has all been discussed, and then discussed again, so that there is really no new ground to cover. The answer is still the same. We are committed to a policy of daylight bombing, and we won't change."

"I didn't really think you would, sir," Percival said. "But I did promise Arthur that I would speak to you."

"You can go back and tell him you spoke to me," General Eaker said. "And you can tell him that the answer is still the same."

"Perhaps you could give me something to take back," Percival said. "Something other than a flat rejection. Perhaps a spirit of cooperation in some venture."

"What exactly do you have in mind?" General Eaker asked.

"I've been thinking about something," Percival said. "Now bear in mind that it is not my job to develop the policy of our air efforts or even to suggest possible targets. But what if the U.S. Air Corps and the R.A.F. selected one particularly important target and then combined their tactics. The R.A.F. could bomb the target by night and your chaps could bomb it by day. After all, Harris is actually just interested in maximizing the effort. Wouldn't that do it?"

Eaker looked at Percival and smiled broadly. "You know something, General? You may just have something there. Yes, sir, you may have just come up with an idea that might work. Curt?"

"Yes, sir?"

"Get with the R.A.F. target acquisition boys and find us a really good show."

"Yes, sir!" Porter said.

"Now," Eaker said, smiling. "We'll do exactly what I told Churchill we would do. We'll keep those bastards awake round the clock."

6

The truck was painted the same shade of field gray and green as all the other German vehicles, but it was completely different in appearance. It was a panel truck with a loop antenna on top. Although it was an innocent-looking vehicle, it was one which could strike terror into the heart of all the 'pianists' working in Paris, for it was loaded with radio equipment that could locate the origin of radio messages.

In the back of the truck a radio operator sat hunched over a control panel laden with all sorts of radio equipment. Behind him was a lieutenant holding the microphone which kept him in touch with the two other similarly equipped trucks cruising the city.

The driver looked over his shoulder at the two men in the back.

"Perhaps she will not transmit today," he suggested.

"She will transmit," the German lieutenant said. "She has transmitted every day at exactly eleven o'clock, and she will transmit today. Carmen is most dependable in this regard."

"What do you think she is like, this Carmen?" the driver asked, as he turned down Rue Mouffetard. A French civilian, seeing the truck, turned his back to it as it drove by him. "Is she beautiful, this one?" He honked impatiently at an old man pushing a cart.

"I think she is a brave, but foolish woman," the lieutenant replied.

"Do you think she is really a woman at all?" the driver asked. "Or a man, using the name of a woman?"

"Carmen is a woman," the radio operator said knowledgeably.

"Oh? How can you be so certain of that?" the driver asked.

"She has the woman's touch on the wireless key," the radio operator said. He searched the dial, turning it slowly through the frequency bands.

The driver laughed. "Are you going to tell

me you can really determine if the operator is a man or a woman just by listening to the wireless key?"

"Yes, of course," the operator said. "Everyone has a distinctive touch, and men and women are different from each other. Carmen is a woman, I can—" suddenly he held up his hand. "Lieutenant! It is her! She is on frequency 119.5!"

"Attention, attention!" the lieutenant said in his microphone. "Unit Two and Unit Three, are you there?"

"Yes, Lieutenant, this is Unit Two, reporting."

"Unit Three, here."

"Tune to frequency 119.5," the German Lieutenant ordered.

"I have a bearing," the radio operator said.

"We *have* her!" the lieutenant said, smiling happily. "As soon as we get another bearing, we can cross the lines, and pick her up. Ah, Carmen, you have led us a merry chase, but this time you lose."

"Lieutenant, this is Unit Two, we cannot raise the signal."

"What? But you must raise the signal; she will not transmit long. Unit Three, have you the signal?"

"No, Lieutenant."

"Lieutenant, you did say 119.5, didn't you?" Unit Two asked.

"Yes," the Lieutenant said, his voice clearly

showing his agitation that the signal had not been raised.

"Lieutenant, I'm sorry," his radio operator suddenly said. "Did I say 119.5? I meant 115.9."

"Dumbhead!" the Lieutenant said angrily. "Correction, correction, it is 115.9, *not* 119.5!" he shouted into his microphone, but even as he spoke, the signal stopped.

"It is too late," the radio operator said. "She has finished her transmission."

"Unit Two, Unit Three, did you get the transmission?"

"No, Lieutenant," Unit Two said.

"I'm sorry," Unit Three reported.

The Lieutenant threw down his microphone in disgust, then took off his cap and rubbed his nearly bald head. His captain would be upset with him. His captain had developed an obsession to find Carmen. He would trade any two agents for Carmen, the lieutenant knew.

"Did you get a bearing?" he asked the radio operator.

"Yes, Lieutenant, but it will do no good," the operator said. He laid a compass and ruler across the street map of Paris, and drew a long blue line. "She is somewhere along this line," he said. "But without a bearing from the other operators, we can't make the lines cross, so we have no idea where she is. She could be anywhere along this line. The chances of our finding her today are quite slim.''

"Yes," the lieutenant said. "And now, I must report to Captain Streicher."

In the staff lounge of a hospital in London, Midge Waverly listened to the evening news.

"This is the BBC Home Service. Here is the news. It was announced today that elements of General Wingate's 77th Indian Infantry Brigade, known for their brilliant sortie far behind Japanese lines in Burma, have gone on the offensive once more. Details were not released, but it was made known today that at least one company has re-entered the Burmese jungle to carry out harassment and communication disrupting tactics.

In other news, Air Chief Marshal Sir Arthur Harris announced today that the spirit of co-operation which exists between the R.A.F. and the Eighth U.S.A.A.F. will ensure the early demise of the German Nation. Bombing around the clock will. . . ."

Midge turned off the news. She had heard the news about Greg, and no other news mattered. Greg, her husband, was a member of Wingate's Indian Infantry Brigade, a ''Chindit'' he called himself. He had hinted in recent letters that he would soon be engaged in a new operation, and

121

she knew that it was his company which had gone behind the Japanese lines.

Midge knew she should feel a great deal of concern for him, but she didn't. She felt guilty about that. After all, she was flying under false colors, purporting to be the brave, supporting wife of one of the Empire's officers away at war. But it had been over two years since she had last seen her husband, and even then the relationship had been severely strained.

Midge was perhaps the most beautiful of the three Cairns-Whiteacre daughters. She was also the oldest, and the most disillusioned.

Midge had been the darling of the social set in pre-war England. She was photographed at the races, cricket matches and polo meets. It was at a polo match that she met, and became infatuated with, a young teamsman from the Indian Army: Lieutenant Gregory Hughes Waverly.

Greg Waverly, like many Englishmen before him, had graduated from Sandhurst, and had received his commission in the Indian Army. Life for an officer in the Indian Army was most grand, and Greg had enjoyed every moment of it.

The infatuation was a two-way affair, and Greg managed to convince Midge that her role as the wife of an officer in the Indian Army would mean excitement and unbelievable luxury. Midge married Greg in what was billed as the wedding of the season.

Things did not go as Midge had hoped. She had been born and raised in luxury, so the plush living conditions were not enough to offset the things about India which she found intolerable. She hated the climate, and she hated the filth and squalor of the cities. She disliked the Indian people, and she was frightened that at any moment India might explode into revolution. She badgered Greg to resign his Indian Army commission and return to England, and when he didn't, she returned without him, telling him that it would only be for a short visit.

The war began while Midge was in England, and that provided her with all the excuse she needed for not going back. Greg managed one brief leave in the meantime, but all other contact between them was through letters.

Sometimes Midge was a little jealous of her sister Karen. Karen's husband Phillip was a bomber pilot in the R.A.F. Midge knew that her sister's husband faced great danger on every mission, and there was always the possibility that he wouldn't return at all. In between missions, though, he was in England, and Karen was able to see him several times a week.

Of course, Allison was the luckiest of the three and the one Midge envied most. Allison had no husband at all. She was free, not only of worry, but also of responsibility, and during a time of abundance—as far as handsome and exciting men went—Allison was able to pick and choose, like a shopper in a mart.

Midge would have given anything to have the freedom of movement Allison enjoyed. She had to be particularly careful, though, because, as the married daughter of the Earl of Dunleigh and the Countess of Warbo, she was highly visible. She had, in fact, already received some criticism about the way she dressed. Midge was proud of her looks, of her blonde hair, which she kept the color of spun gold, and her shapely, statuesque figure. She had her nurse's uniforms tailored to show off that figure to its best advantage, and she wore makeup, even when she was working.

Her sister Karen had mentioned once, during a visit, some talk she had heard about Midge's mode of dress. Midge countered by saying that the wounded soldiers deserved to see the nurses looking their best. It was generally agreed that having a nurse as beautiful as Midge was good for their morale, so the talk finally stopped.

Midge liked to pretend that the gossip meant nothing to her, but it did. In fact, though she would have loved to go out on an innocent date— just dinner and dancing—she would never be able to do so. She was much too well known and in the public eye for that. Therefore, though she was asked out at least three times a week, she always had to turn the invitations down.

The door to the nurses' break-room swung open,

and a doctor stepped inside. He saw Midge and smiled.

"Ah, so there you are," he said. "I was afraid you were gone."

"Dr. Thompson, were you looking for me? I'm sorry. I just wanted to catch the home service news on BBC."

"Are we still marching forward to sure and certain victory?" Dr. Thompson asked, mimicking the resonant tones of a radio announcer's voice.

"Quite," Midge answered. "Hand in hand with the Americans, of course."

"Of course," Dr. Thompson said, and they both laughed.

"Did you need something?" Midge asked.

"Yes, actually. Would you be a dear and lend me a hand? Busy hands are happy hands, you know, and every effort helps to hurt the Hun and slap the Jap, as they say."

"Of course, Doctor Thompson, I'll be glad to assist you," Midge said. She stood and smoothed the skirt of her uniform.

"Doctor Thompson, is it? I thought we had gone beyond all that. Weren't you calling me Teddy?"

"I'm sorry if I was too forward," Midge apologized.

"Forward? Not at all, dear girl. Not at all," Teddy said. He looked at Midge, and for just a second his eyes reflected his appreciation of her striking beauty. Midge basked in the warm glow

125

of that realization; then, rather than let him see the effect it was having on her, she cleared her throat.

"What task do you have in mind?" she asked.

"I'm going to make the rounds in Q Ward," he said.

"Oh, Teddy, no," Midge said. "Do I have to? I mean, isn't there someone else you could ask? I really don't like it in Q Ward."

'Q' Ward was where the most seriously wounded were being cared for, and though it was depressing to see any of the wounded young men who were being treated at the hospital, it was acutely depressing to visit Q Ward.

"Midge, I chose you for a special reason," Teddy said. "The poor blokes in Q have little enough to look forward to during the day as it is. You are able to bring a little cheer to an otherwise despondent group of young men."

"I know I shouldn't feel this way," Midge said. "After all, if they can live with their wounds, I should at least be able to look at them."

"That's my girl," Teddy said. "Now, do come along, won't you?"

Midge followed the doctor down the long, dimly lit corridor, then up the back stairs to the fourth floor. There was a sign on a stand just outside the swinging doors which led into the hospital ward:

Q Ward
Seriously Wounded
"A" Badge required

126

Doctor Thompson pushed the doors open, and he and Midge entered the ward. There was a long row of beds down each side of the ward, some of which were separated by screens. On each bed lay a terribly disfigured or maimed piece of humanity. There were men without legs or arms and others with terrible burns and scars. Midge felt an uneasy sensation as she walked along with the doctor. The eyes of all the men followed her quietly and, it seemed to her, sullenly.

"Doctor Thompson," she said uneasily. "I don't think I should be in here. These men. . . ."

"Easy, nurse," the doctor said. "Don't worry about it. It will be all right, just trust me."

"I don't think so," Midge said. She looked around at the quiet, staring, almost accusing eyes. "I think these men . . . resent me."

"Nonsense," the doctor said. He stopped at the foot of one of the beds. The man in the bed was wrapped in bandages from his chest up. Both arms were bandaged and suspended from an overhead pulley. His face, except for his eyes, was wrapped with only a small hole for a mouth and another for his nose.

"So, how are we today?" Doctor Thompson asked, stopping at the wounded man's bed.

"We are fine," the man mumbled from behind his bandages.

"That's wonderful," Doctor Thompson said. "Nurse, this is Flight Sergeant Alexander Morris," he said with exaggerated good humor. "He was flying as a gunner in a Lancaster bomber when a kraut anti-aircraft shell burst in his lap. The lads with him gave him first aid, brought him home, and here he is. We'll fix him up as good as new."

"I'm goin' to get a new face," the patient said. His words were mumbled from behind the wrappings, and Midge leaned forward.

"What did you say?"

"I'm goin' to get a bleedin' new face," the sergeant said again. "I'm goin' to pick one out, like pickin' out a suit. It's goin' to be 'ansome this time. Not like the ugly mug I left back in Germany."

Midge looked over at Doctor Thompson in surprise.

"Well, you know they can do wonders with plastic surgery nowadays," Doctor Thompson said. "And though his face was virtually blown away, much of the bone structure remained intact. I think he will be quite pleasantly surprised."

" 'Ave you seen any o' the faces the doctors 'ave made, Miss?" Sergeant Morris asked in an innocent voice.

"No," Midge said. "No, I haven't, but I'm certain they are quite nice," she added, not knowing what else to say.

"They look like a bleedin' arse with eyes," Sergeant Morris said, his tone suddenly and unexpectedly changing from deceptive innocence to angry derision.

"Sergeant Morris, I'll have you know this is Lady Margaret Whiteacre-Waverly. You've no cause to be rude in front of her," Doctor Thompson said angrily.

"If she's a Lady like you say, what the bloody 'ell is she doin' in 'ere?"

"She's a volunteer nurse, offering her services. Instead of being rude to her, you should be thankful that a woman such as Lady Margaret has taken it upon herself to dedicate her time to men such as you."

"I've got nothin' to thank the Lady for, Doc," Sergeant Morris said. "No, nor anyone else in the bleedin' Q Ward. Look at 'er, struttin' around here with 'er tits a-bouncin', gettin' the men all worked up, knowin' there's not a thing in the world any of us can do about it. You should come in here some night after she leaves. All the beds start squeakin' and shakin' while the men relieve themselves."

Midge gasped.

"Sergeant! That is quite enough!" Doctor Thompson said sharply.

"Oh, is it, now?" Sergeant Morris said. "Tell me, Doc—jus' what in the bloody 'ell are you goin' to do to me? Put me in solitary? You think I got no right to be upset? Listen, let me tell you somethin'. Let me tell you a few of the facts of life. At least these other men can flog their doggins after *Lady* Margaret prances around in front of 'em. I can't even do that. I got no 'ands, you see. I got no 'ands at all. I got to just lie 'ere 'n suffer.''

"I . . . I'm sorry," Midge said. She was crying now, and she took several steps away from the Sergeant's bunk, then looked up and down the ward at the others. They were still looking at her with accusing eyes, but now, strangely, some of the eyes reflected a sense of victory, as if they had been vindicated by the Sergeant's angry words.

"Nurse, don't let this bother you," Doctor Thompson said.

"I . . . I had no idea," Midge said, walking quickly out of the ward and blinded by the tears which stung her eyes.

"Nurse," Dr. Thompson called to her. "Midge! Come back! Don't let him get to you like that!''

"I'm sorry!" Midge called back, as she hurried down the stairs outside the ward.

Teddy came down to the staff lounge several minutes later to talk to Midge.

"Perhaps I should explain a few things to you," he said. "About men and their sexual needs.''

"You needn't explain anything to me," Midge said. "After all, I am a married woman.''

"I know," Teddy said. "And I've no doubt that your . . . uh, married life has been quite normal and satisfying. But that is the very reason you must have a few things explained to you. I hope you will listen to me and bear with me, for it might get a little indelicate.''

''Go on.''

''Now, it is true that some men can go their entire lives without sexual outlet. There are, of course, men who take vows of celibacy, though some suspect that many of these men must occasionally resort to . . . uh, well, there is no delicate way of putting it . . . masturbation. Without masturbation and the occasional release of semen through nocturnal emission, it would be impossible for those men to function. Do you know what nocturnal emission is?''

''I can imagine,'' Midge said. ''I suppose it means having sexual release at night.''

''Yes, while asleep. The slang term for it is 'wet dream.' Now, in teen-agers, before sexual experience, and in adults who are celibate, nocturnal emissions occur naturally and spontaneously. However, in healthy young males who have been sexually active, such occurrences are rare. That is because there are other ways of relieving the pressure, either through normal sexual outlets or by masturbation. In the event that *both* outlets are denied to an otherwise healthy young male, nocturnal emission is the *only* way, and since such emissions are not normal to the healthy male, they must be stimulated. Do you understand what I'm trying to say?''

"I'm not sure," Midge said, though a nagging feeling began to pull at her.

"Quite simply, Midge, you are the therapy. If Sergeant Morris sees you often enough, and becomes stimulated . . ."

"Stimulated? You mean *aroused?* Doctor Thompson, what are you saying? Am I being used as . . . as bait?"

"In a sense, you might say that," Teddy admitted.

"How *could* you do such a thing?" Midge asked.

"I'm sorry, Midge," Teddy apologized quickly. "But you must try to understand. Unless Sergeant Morris is sufficiently stimulated to fantasize about you, he will not be able to activate the mechanism which triggers nocturnal emission. This is a very necessary therapy, as important to his recovery as any other care we can provide for him."

"All right," Midge said quietly. "But what about Sergeant Morris?"

"What about him?" Teddy asked.

"Isn't this hard on him? You heard what he said up there. Never mind the degradation such 'therapy' makes me feel. What about Sergeant Morris? Do you really think this is fair to him?"

"It is the only way," Teddy replied. "I will admit to you that it is an extremely difficult way. Actually, it is a rather exquisite form of torture for him. But it is often the case that cures are as painful as the malady they are designed to correct, and this is just such a case.''

''I see,'' Midge said.

''Then you do forgive me?'' Teddy asked, with an expression of concern on his face.

''I . . . don't know,'' Midge said. ''I think I can forgive you for what this does to me, but it's Sergeant Morris I'm worried about.''

''If you think about it, I'm sure you'll realize that in the long run this is the only way.'' Teddy put his hand on her shoulder. ''Midge, sometimes convention and rules must be circumvented if results are to be achieved. And in times of war, that holds true more than ever. You just think about it for a while. You'll see that I am right.''

''I'll think about it, Teddy,'' Midge promised.

''Good, good,'' Teddy said. He rubbed his hands together, then looked up at the clock on the lounge wall. ''Well, I see it is nearly ten, and I've not yet had my dinner. Won't you join me?''

''I have duty until midnight,'' Midge explained.

''Oh? Well, perhaps after you finish your duty we could get together for a drink. That's only two more hours, and I would be happy to wait for you.''

''No,'' Midge said. ''Thank you for the invitation, Teddy. Perhaps some other time, but not now.''

Teddy smiled at the realization that she had left the door open to the possibility of another time.

"Well then, I shall try again," he said. "Good night, Midge. Don't let what happened here tonight disturb you."

"Good night," Midge said.

Midge walked out to the nurse's station and took her seat. From here she could monitor the light board, should she be summoned by any of the patients. Here, also, she could answer the telephone and admit new patients, should admission be required.

Midge stayed at her station for nearly an hour after Doctor Thompson left. She could see down the long, dark corridors which led from her station to the various wards, and she could see the night lamps burning over the doors of the rooms which were occupied.

It was quiet. A water cooler gurgled, and a clock ticked away the time. Somewhere in the distance Midge heard a train. She was alone with her thoughts.

The more she thought about it, the more sympathy she developed for Sergeant Morris's plight. She thought of his hollow, haunted voice and the accusing eyes of the others in Q Ward, and she wanted to cry for his pain.

At 2315 hours, forty-five minutes before midnight, Midge put up a sign on her desk. The sign said "Making Rounds," and it would authorize her thirty minutes away from her station. Should any patient need her during that time, there were call boards located strategically throughout the hospital, and she could check them periodically to see if she were being summoned. A gently ringing bell would call her attention to one of the boards.

Midge climbed the back stairs to the fourth floor, then stood outside the door to Q Ward for a long moment. Then she took a deep breath, as if she were about to plunge into cold water, and stepped inside.

Everyone in the ward was asleep. She could hear their measured, and sometimes labored, breathing as she walked quietly between the two rows of beds. She reached Sergeant Morris's bed. A splash of moonlight spilled in from the window and bathed the sleeping figure in silver.

Midge looked at him, at his arms and chest and head all wrapped and bound in bandage and gauze. Her heart went out to him, and she stepped up to his bed.

"Sergeant Morris," she called softly.

The sleeping figure groaned once.

"Sergeant Morris," Midge called again. "Please wake up."

Sergeant Morris stirred, then there was a movement, a flutter, beneath the bandage around his head. There were holes in the bandage where his eyes were, and those two holes seemed to stare at her. She could almost imagine there was anger in those holes.

"What is it?" Sergeant Morris asked. "What do you want?"

"I wanted to tell you I'm sorry," Midge said. "I'm sorry about—"

"You woke me up for that?" Sergeant Morris said angrily.

Midge felt the tears leap to her eyes, and she turned her head away from the terrible, accusing stare of those hollow holes.

"Ah, listen," Sergeant Morris said, and the tone of his voice was softened, more conciliatory. "What are you sorry about anyway? Are you sorry because you are so pretty? You can't 'elp that."

"I'm sorry about your . . . your condition," Midge said.

"Yeah?" Sergeant Morris said. "Well, you can't 'elp that either."

"Maybe I can," Midge said quietly.

"What? What are you talkin' about?"

"I can't help your condition, but I can help what you were so upset about today."

"How?"

"Shh," Midge warned. "Be quiet." She stuck her hand under the bed clothes and slipped it down across Sergeant Morris's stomach. He was wearing nothing from the waist down, just as Midge had known.

"What are you doin'?" Sergeant Morris hissed.

"Shh!" Midge said again. She wrapped her fingers around him and felt it growing, literally leaping to her touch. It felt hot. It felt so incredibly hot.

"My God, miss! Do . . . do you know what you are doin'?" Sergeant Morris gasped. He was just barely able to get the words out.

"Just lie back," Midge commanded. She spoke quietly and authoritatively. "Just lie back and relax."

Midge began moving her hand up and down, feeling the hot, smooth skin beneath her fingers. She moved her hand skillfully and, in a very real way, lovingly, for she was answering a compulsion which had driven her from the moment she became aware of the sergeant's condition.

Sergeant Morris began to breathe in more labored gasps, and Midge could feel the muscles in his stomach tense and strain, then grow incredibly hard.

"You'd . . . you'd better stop," Sergeant Morris gasped. "You'd better stop before . . . before I. . . ."

"Go ahead," Midge said. "Let it happen, Sergeant." She increased her efforts, working with quick, sensual strokes, gentle and yet demanding.

"I, uh, oh, oh, oh," Sergeant Morris said, grunting and groaning with each hot spurt. Midge continued to work her hand, feeling the hot wetness which cascaded down over her fingers until, finally, the spurting stopped. She held on for a moment longer, squeezing gently, but firmly, until the last twitching movement stopped and Sergeant Morris began to relax, to grow flaccid in her tender grasp. When finally she released him, Midge used the wash basin and cloth to clean him tenderly and with concern.

Sergeant Morris didn't say a word until the basin was returned to the bedside table and the cloth was dropped into the laundry bag. Then he mumbled something, but Midge couldn't hear, and she had to lean close.

"What did you say?" Midge asked.

"I said, thanks." Sergeant Morris said in a choked voice, and then Midge realized that he was crying.

7

Linda sat on the toilet in the bathroom in her tiny flat in Paris. Above her head was the flush chain of the toilet, and attached to it, so that the chain itself became part of the antenna, was the transmitting aerial. Linda sent out a three-letter code to establish contact.

Her earphones clicked an answer, and Linda went to work. She requested additional explosives for the underground and gave the coordinates as to where they were to be delivered. She did it all in code-letter groupings, so the entire message took but a few seconds.

Linda knew about the radio direction finders the

139

Germans were using all over the city. She knew that as soon as two or more stations picked up her signal, it would be a simple matter of triangulation to find her, so she managed to keep her message incredibly brief.

The Germans had no way of tracing the messages which were coming in from London, though, so it was not necessary for London to be as cryptic. As soon as Linda finished her message, she signalled that she was ready for London's reply.

"Attention, Carmen, be advised that three stations in your net have been discovered and neutralized. It is possible that the entire network has been endangered. Do not acknowledge this transmission now. In your next transmission, include information as to where and when you can be withdrawn. In the interest of your safety, you are returning to England."

"No," Linda said aloud. "No, I can't return to England. There is too much to do here."

Linda disconnected the radio, then dismantled it and put it in the bicycle seat. The bicycle seat made the perfect cover for her. When she was away from her apartment, she had the radio with her, so any surprise search wouldn't turn the instrument up. When she was home, she removed the bicycle seat as a precaution against bicycle theft, and thus had the radio instrument with her at all times.

140

Linda flushed the toilet, as if to give some validity to her being there, then left the bathroom and closed the door behind her. Quickly, she got ready to leave her apartment. She had to go to Marcel's Cafe, not only to report on the results of her communication with London, but also to see if there were any new requirements for her services.

"Ahh, Fraulein Ben-Ahr, are you going out?" Major Goethe asked as Linda stepped out into the hallway. Major Goethe lived in the apartment across from Linda's. He was fat, and he smelled of garlic. He was assigned to the German military film archives, and he had once confided to Linda that he had been a film director before the war.

"Not a very famous director, you understand," he had told her, "but a director with pride in my art. I had dreams of some day coming to Paris to make a great movie, one which would be acclaimed by critics around the world. Instead, I come to Paris to film parades. *Parades,* Kani . . . the would-be-great Ernst Goethe is filming *parades.*"

Linda recalled the conversation, and she flashed a big smile. Major Goethe was not a dangerous man; in fact, she rather liked him.

"I'm going to Marcel's, Ernst," she said, using his first name. "Perhaps you would like to join me there?"

"Ah, that is a wonderful idea," Goethe enthused.

"But I see you have your bicycle seat with you. Leave it, and we shall go in my car."

"No," Linda said. "I've a few errands to run afterward. I really should take my bicycle. I'll meet you there."

"Nonsense," Goethe said. "We'll simply put your bicycle in the back of the car. How would that be?"

"That would be fine," Linda said, and she smiled. She knew that traveling in the company of a German officer would decrease the chances of a sudden unexpected search.

Linda walked down the stairs with Goethe and stood by as he loaded her bicycle into the back seat of his open staff car. When the bicycle was loaded, he held the door open for her. Then he climbed in himself, and they drove off toward the cafe.

Marcel's was a cafe with a sidewalk terrace. It had been a favorite meeting place for such people as Ernest Hemingway, F. Scott Fitzgerald, Gertrude Stein, Ezra Pound, and Ford Madox Ford before the war, and thus it had acquired an international reputation as a cafe which was favored by artists. Miguel LeGrand, a French writer who was a close personal friend of Ernest Hemingway and whose own work was often compared with Hemingway's, was the only writer from the original "Papa's Cadre" who still frequented the cafe. He had been paroled out of a German prisoner of war camp right after France capitulated.

The cafe was now a favorite among those German officers who considered themselves artists, writers or poets in their own right. It was a natural for Goethe, who thought of himself as a movie director first and a German officer second.

What Goethe and the other Germans who frequented the cafe did not know was that the cafe was also the headquarters for a major underground army corps. They would have been surprised to learn that Marcel Garneau, who owned the cafe, and Miguel LeGrand, its most famous patron, were both high-ranking, active officers in the Free French Underground.

It was nearly noon when Goethe and Linda arrived. The tables were crowded with German officers and French women, but Marcel, declaring Goethe and Linda to be two of his favorite people, managed to find a place for them.

"Is Miguel around?" Goethe asked.

"No, I'm sorry, Major, he is not in now," Marcel answered. "I expect he will be in before the day is over. He visits us every day."

"He is a fine writer," remarked Goethe. "I say this, and I say it without hesitation: I respect his work, and I think it is folly to ban his books in Germany. When they burned his books, along with the works of Hemingway, Steinbeck and Orwell, I wanted to weep. Yes, I did, I really wanted to weep. I look forward to the day when this war is ended and all the paranoia is placed behind us. I very much want to produce a film from one of Miguel's books.''

''I'm certain Miguel would be most interested in talking with you about that,'' Marcel said.

''What about you, Kani? Don't you find Miguel's books fascinating?''

''I have not read too many,'' Linda said. ''And what I have read, I find a bit too robust for my taste.''

Goethe laughed. ''Robust, yes! They are robust . . . and quite sexy, too!''

''Will you take lunch today, Major Goethe? I have received some marvelous sausages from a few friends.''

''Sausages?'' Goethe exclaimed, rubbing his stomach appreciatively. ''Oh my, you have sausages?''

''Yes, indeed,'' Marcel said. ''I'll bring you some.''

''Good, good. Kani, you must be my guest and eat with me,'' Goethe invited.

''Thank you,'' Linda said. ''But first I must see Chantal. She was going to locate some pencils for my sketching. Marcel, is Chantal here?''

''She is in the kitchen, Kani,'' Marcel said easily.

Linda excused herself, and strolled back to the kitchen. Then, when she received the 'all clear' from one of the cooks, she disappeared behind a brick wall by slipping through a section which opened, then closed in such a way that anyone who saw the wall would never realize that it concealed a secret passage.

Behind the wall was a small room, and in the room a handful of men and one woman were busy putting food and supplies into baskets for the secret armies in the hills.

Miguel embraced Linda in greeting, and so did Chantal. Chantal was Marcel's twenty-four-year-old daughter. She was tall and blonde, and looked remarkably like her father.

"The explosives will be here as you ordered," Linda said. "They will be dropped by parachute at the designated coordinates."

"Good, good," Miguel said. "Now, you must tell them that we have rescued the American crew of a B-17. The pilot's name is Captain Martin Holt. Send the message immediately, so we can arrange for their pickup. And yours."

"My pickup?" Linda asked.

"Kani, did you not get the message from London that you were to be picked up and returned?" Miguel asked.

"Yes," Linda said. "But I don't wish to go."

"Tell her, Miguel," Chantal said. "Tell her what we have discovered."

"Tell me what?"

Miguel looked at Linda, then he looked down

145

sadly. "The Germans have found two more pianists," he said. "You are the only one left in our network."

"That's all the more reason I should stay," Linda said.

"Kani, don't you understand? The Germans killed both operators. Now the reward for Carmen has been raised. Everyone in the city will be looking for you."

"If I am gone, who will arrange for your supplies?" Linda asked. "If I weren't here, who would arrange for the rescue of the American fliers like the crew you have just saved?"

"Go back to England," Chantal pleaded. "Don't worry about such things now."

"Go back with the American crew," Miguel said.

"Look, Miguel, Chantal, I knew this would be a difficult job when I accepted it," Linda said. "I'm not going to run now, not just because it is beginning to get a little rougher."

"If you go back, I'm certain a new network will be put in place," Miguel suggested.

"I am certain they are already beginning to put a new network in place," Linda said. "But there will be requirements in the meantime. I shall stay and fulfill those requirements. Don't worry—I'll be even more careful than before. I will not signal from the same location two times in a row."

"Good girl," Miguel said.

"When I tell London of the American air crew, I will tell them also that I am staying," Linda said.

The brick wall opened, and Marcel stepped inside.

"Kani, Goethe is asking about you. He is complaining that he can't look at your sausages much longer without losing his will power and taking them for himself."

Linda laughed. "I'd better get back. I'm not worried about his will power, but I wouldn't want to alert his suspicion. I will tell London of the air crew."

"Be careful," Miguel warned.

Linda returned to the table. All of Goethe's sausages were gone, and he was looking hungrily at those on Linda's plate.

"Oh heavens," Linda said. "I could never eat this many. Ernst, you will be a dear and help me, won't you?"

Goethe's face lit up in a big smile, and he reached for a generous portion.

"Of course, of course, Fraulein, anything for a beautiful lady."

Linda watched him as he began to devour his unexpected bounty, and then she knew how she would continue her work. She would plant her radio sender in Goethe's car. Her sending schedule would, of necessity, be erratic, but with the collapse of the network the schedules would be

147

scrapped anyway. And the erratic schedule would more than be offset by the advantages gained. The car would be constantly on the move and make a radio position fix difficult to obtain. And it was the car of a German officer, an unlikely place for the authorities to search.

She smiled. It would work. She knew it would.

8

Allison walked over to the ready-desk to turn in her keys. The shift boss took the keys, then looked up. Recognizing Allison, she shoved a note across the desk toward her.

"You've been getting telephone calls from Elaine Standridge," the woman said. "I don't know what she wants, but she's been quite insistent. She even wanted me to send someone to track you down."

"Thank you, Mrs. Pinkham," Allison said. "She works in the Rainbow Corner; I'll just pop in and see what she wants."

Allison had never been inside the Rainbow Corner. The gauntlet of American soldiers she had to run every time she walked by the place had been all the discouragement she'd needed. She avoided the place like the plague when she could. But it was very unlike Elaine to try with such determination to reach her, so it had to be something important. Because of that, Allison was willing, and able, to repress her aversion to the seamier aspects of the place and go inside.

Inside the Rainbow Corner the air was heavy with coffee and tobacco smoke. There were literally hundreds of soldiers sitting around or standing in little groups, talking and laughing. There were a few card games in progress, and here and there someone was reading a book, but in most cases the groups of men were congregated around girls, generally at a ratio of fifteen or twenty to one.

The biggest single group was gathered around a piano, which one American soldier was playing in accompaniment to the loud and rather off-key singing of an impromptu chorus section. They were singing *Mairzy Doats and Dozy Doats,* the totally nonsensical American song which had become so popular during the American 'invasion' of England.

One of the girls around whom a large contingent of soldiers stood was a very pretty blonde. Allison walked over to her.

"Elaine, I got the message that you wanted to see me," Allison said.

Elaine had been laughing at something one of the soldiers had said, but when she looked up and saw

150

Allison, the smile left her face and a clouded expression came across her eyes. The change in her expression frightened Allison.

"Elaine, what is it?" Allison asked. "What's wrong?"

"Let's go into my office," Elaine said, walking away from the others toward a small room nearby. Allison followed her into the office, and Elaine pulled the door shut.

"Do you know the Yank I sent home to my room, but who wound up in your room by mistake?"

"Martin Holt?" Allison said. "Yes, of course. What about him?"

"I've received some rather distressing news."

"Elaine, what is it?" Allison asked again. "My God, is he all right? Is he . . . is he *dead?*"

"No, nothing like that," Elaine said. She put her hand comfortingly on Allison's. "Oh my, he did get through to you, didn't he? He is a handsome devil, I'll give you that." Elaine waited for a moment, then took a deep breath. "He's been shot down."

"Shot down? Where? Is he all right?"

"All I was able to find out was that he was shot down. The person who told me said he believed Martin crash-landed in France. If that is true, there may be a chance. I wish I could tell you more, but I honestly don't know any more than that. Allison, if I had known, if I had realized how important this young man really was to you, I would have tried to find out more. I'm sorry."

"I didn't know myself how important he was until right now," Allison said. "I'll find out about him. This is where I discover whether being the daughter of a general has any advantages."

Allison sat in the car in front of Eighth U.S.A.A.F. Headquarters, where her father was occupied inside. She had called him as soon as she'd heard about Martin, and had begged him to come to London to find out what he could. Her father had expressed some curiosity as to why she should be so concerned about the fate of an American flier, but he agreed to do what he could, and Allison managed to draw the assignment to drive him around as he looked into the situation.

General Sir Percival Cairns-Whiteacre had been inside the building for nearly an hour. Allison would have given anything in the world to be inside with him now, but security was too tight. She had to stay in the car until they left the American compound.

Allison drummed her fingers on the steering wheel and watched the guards marching back and forth on their posts. She wished she could get out and march with them, for the pacing would surely make the waiting easier.

Finally, after an interminable length of time, her father came back outside and walked over to the car. He climbed into the front seat next to Allison.

"What did you find out?" Allison asked him before he'd even had time to shut the door.

"He's alive," Percival said, smiling broadly at his daughter. "He's alive and he's unhurt."

"Oh, thank God," Allison said. She laughed and cried at the same time. "Oh, thank God," she said again. "Where is he? Is he a prisoner?"

"First, I want to know why you have such an intense interest in this American flier," Percival said. "See here, Allison, are you and Captain Holt lovers?"

"No," Allison said. "Actually, I've only met him once."

"Once, and you show this much concern?"

"He made a lasting impression on me," Allison said.

"I can see that he did," Percival said. "But you are going to have to give me more than that, daughter. I've moved mountains to find out about him, and you've put me in somewhat of a spot. I'm at least going to have the satisfaction of knowing why. Are you in love with him?"

Allison laughed. "In love with him? Father, I told you, I only met him once. How could I be?"

"Yes," Percival said. "How could you be?"

Allison sighed. "I honestly don't know, Father. Is it possible to fall in love so quickly? I can't explain it, but when I heard from Elaine that he had been shot down, I felt such an overwhelming sense of grief and loss. Maybe there is something brewing, and maybe not. It's hard for me to say. I am so thankful now that I know he is alive and well. I can only hope that he survives prison camp.''

"He's lucky on that score as well," Percival said. "He isn't in prison camp at all. He was picked up by a French Underground unit. One of our radio contacts in Paris has already made the arrangements. He will be back in England at 0200 hours in the morning.''

"He's . . . he's coming back? Tonight?''

"Yes," Percival said. "The Americans are sending a Dakota for Captain Holt and his crew.''

"Oh, thank you, Father!" Allison said happily, and she threw her arms around his neck and kissed him soundly.

"Here, here," Percival said, coughing and extracting himself from his daughter's embrace. "Do you want to cause talk?''

Allison giggled. "You're my father! Let them talk all they want.''

"They don't know that you're my daughter," Percival said. "They see only a beautiful young driver and a stodgy old general. After all, look at the talk which is already going around about the American General Eisenhower and his driver. I don't want to get into that pot of tea, no sir.''

"I met Miss Summersby," Allison said. "And believe me, it is much more Kay's doing than General Eisenhower's. Besides, there is really nothing going on.''

"Nevertheless, there is talk," Percival said.

"Father, I want you to do one more thing for me."

"And that is?"

"I want you to find out where his plane will land, and fix it so I can be there to meet him."

"Daughter, you ask the impossible," Percival complained. "Now, if he were a British flier, I could arrange it. But he's American. I can't just snap my fingers like that and—"

"Try," Allison said. "You can at least try, can't you?"

Percival looked at his daughter for a long time, then a slow smile began spreading across his face.

Suddenly Allison realized why he was smiling, and she let out a little sound of joy. "Oh, Father, you've already done it, haven't you? You have already fixed things. I *am* going to be there to meet him!"

"I thought you would scarcely go to all this trouble unless you wanted to be there when he came back," Percival said. "So I did make the arrangements. You will be my driver for the next twenty-four hours, and we'll go to the airbase to meet him. Of course, if it were up to you, I suppose you would prefer to fly across the Channel in the Dakota that picks him up."

"Oh, Father, could I?"

"No!" Percival said resoundingly. "Absolutely not! You shall have to satisfy yourself with the fact that you will be there when his plane lands."

"I'm satisfied, Father," Allison said with a laugh. "Believe me, I am quite satisfied."

That airplane known to the British as the 'Dakota' was called the 'C-47' by the American military, and the 'DC-3' by the American airlines. A good sized, twin-engined airplane, it is capable of carrying thirty passengers under its military configuration. To fly an airplane that large over enemy territory without being detected, and to land it at night in a field without a paved runway or proper lighting, was no easy task. There was great potential danger for the crew of airplane and also for those who were waiting on the ground. Such an operation had to be completed quickly, lest a German patrol get wind of it and launch a fast surprise attack.

Linda, Chantal and Miguel were at the edge of the large field waiting for the American plane. A runway of sorts was marked by long rows of battery-powered lights. The lights, which were weighted with small sandbags, were not on now, but when Miguel gave the word, his men would dash down each side of the runway and switch them on one at a time.

Linda's job was crucial, for she was manning a small radio. When she heard a signal from the approaching airplane, she would activate the carrier wave only, and the plane's radio compass would home in. Of course, the Germans would be able to home in with a radio compass, too, and that was what made everything so dangerous.

"Kani," Chantal said, using Linda's cover name, which was the only name she knew for her. "When the plane leaves, I still think you should be on it."

"No," Linda said. "We've been through all this, Chantal. I'm staying. I told you, I have a foolproof plan. No one will find my radio."

A man dressed in black, and whose face was blackened in the same way as the other three, trotted up to them.

"Everyone is in place, *mon capitaine*," the man said to Miguel.

"They know the signal for lighting the runway?" Miguel asked the runner, a man named Claude.

"*Oui*. When the first light goes on here, that is when the others will turn on the rest of them."

"Good, good," Miguel said. He looked up toward a small ridge line at the far end. The ridge line made the air operations part of the exercise dangerous, for it rose out of the dark and the pilot of the Dakota would have to have enough altitude to clear it when he took off for the return to England. But it had the advantage of shielding the field from casual observation from the main road. Miguel had guards on the top of the hill to watch the main road for any sign of Germans. There were relatively few German patrols in the area—another reason this field had been chosen.

"Where are the American fliers?" Miguel asked.

"Safe," his runner reported. "They are waiting at the edge of the woods. They will come out only when the door of the plane has been opened, as planned."

"Then everything is well taken care of," Miguel said. "And it will go quite smoothly, yes?" He smiled, and his teeth shone exceptionally white against his darkened face.

"Someday you will write of this, Miguel, and you will be rich and famous," Linda teased.

"I am already rich and famous," Miguel said. "And I would trade it all to see the Boche leave France."

Suddenly Linda got an intense expression on her face, and she adjusted the earphones to her head.

"Is it the plane?" Miguel asked.

"Yes," Linda answered.

"Chantal, stand by the first light," Miguel ordered, and the girl moved quickly to the small lamp at the head of the improvised runway. "Claude, go to the Americans and make certain they are ready."

The runner left to do Miguel's bidding, and Miguel stood by silently and watched Linda as she listened to the approaching plane's radio signal.

"I'm activating the carrier wave now," she said, and she depressed a switch.

"What does that do?" Miguel asked.

"It sends out a radio signal," Linda explained. "If I were sending a message, either by code or by voice, it would be going over that signal. Even though I am sending no message, the radio wave which carries the message is still being transmitted, and that carrier wave will activate the aircraft's homing device.''

"And that of the Germans?''

"Yes,'' Linda admitted. "But without an audible signal it is less likely the Germans will pick up the transmission. Our people can because they know the frequency to monitor.''

"Miguel, I can hear the plane's motors,'' Chantal called.

"Light the runway,'' Miguel ordered, and Chantal turned on the small lamp at her feet.

After Chantal's lamp was turned on, all the others flicked on one at a time as the runners went from one to another. In less than a minute, two rows of dim, but visible lights traced out a runway across the dark field. Miguel and his men had walked that runway a dozen times over the last few hours. They'd removed any rock larger than a lemon, filled in the holes and made certain that there was nothing to provide an unpleasant surprise for the pilot.

The plane touched down at the far end of the field and rolled quickly up to the rear end. It turned, and the side door dropped down. Miguel looked toward the trees and saw the American aviators running to the plane. They were bent low and moving quickly. Just before the last figure got onto the plane, he turned toward Miguel and waved his arm over his head. Miguel waved back at him, and the man climbed on, then pulled the door shut behind him. The pilot increased the throttle, and the plane was rolling, gathering speed quickly. The moment its wheels left the ground, the runway monitor nearest the plane turned off his light. The others followed suit, and the field quickly became dark again.

"Come," Miguel said, as the sound of the airplane's engines receded. "We have done a good job here tonight."

It was damp, and as Allison stood on the tarmac waiting for the plane, she had to wipe her nose several times. She giggled, almost hysterical with the joy of the moment.

"I don't know what he'll think," Allison said. "I will be greeting him with a running nose."

"I should think he would be quite happy to see anyone at all," Percival said, "running nose or not. After all, he did have a very close call."

"Is it much longer?"

"Well, they said two o'clock, but this isn't exactly a scheduled airliner we are waiting for, you know."

"But, Father, you don't think anything could be wrong, do you?"

"Nothing has gone wrong," Percival assured her. "We've already received word that the plane has cleared the coast of France. In fact, it has picked up a fighter escort. Don't worry, it will be here.''

Suddenly the runway lights were turned on and sent out a string of fuzzy jewels that stretched into the distance.

''Oh, the runway lights!'' Allison said. ''They've turned them on!''

''The plane must be near,'' Percival said. ''I expect it is only a few moments now.''

They were quiet, then Allison heard the unmistakeable sound of airplane engines.

''I hear it!'' Allison said. ''Oh, Father, I can hear the plane!''

''There it is, miss,'' a nearby soldier said, overhearing Allison's anxious words and understanding that she had a particular interest in the safe arrival.

''Where?'' Allison asked, looking, straining into the darkness. ''I don't see any lights.''

''He's not showing lights,'' the soldier explained. ''But if you look real close, you can see the exhaust flame. See? The little spot of blue?''

''No,'' Allison said, disappointed that the soldier could see it and she couldn't. Then she saw it. It was a tiny light, no brighter than a star, but moving directly toward them. ''Oh, yes, I can see it now,'' she said. ''See, Father, there it is!''

Allison watched the tiny blue flame until the dark shadow of the airplane itself could be seen. The airplane slipped down out of the darkness, then became visible in the misty, halo-like glare of the runway lights. It floated majestically above the runway for a while, then the tires squealed sharply and made chirping noises as the wheels touched the paved runway.

The plane taxied down the runway, then turned off it and moved toward them. Now it was in the glare of the lights, and Allison could see it clearly. She saw the face of someone through one of the windows, but she couldn't tell if it was Martin.

The engines roared a bit louder as the plane turned into a position with the door facing Allison and the others. When the engines stopped, the propellers continued to turn silently for a bit before finally swinging to a stop. The door was dropped down and a boarding ladder was put in place. In a long moment when nothing seemed to be happening, Allison wanted to scream at them to hurry up, but she remained still.

Finally, a man stood in the doorway, blinking at the lights. There was a light applause for him from those who had gathered at the field, and he smiled and waved. Another man appeared behind him, and then another.

"Where is he?" Allison asked. "Has something gone wrong? Father, are you sure he is on this plane? Are you absolutely *certain?*"

"Relax," Percival said gently. "I'm sure he is on board. If he were not, we would have heard something."

Another man stood in the doorway, also blinking against the bright lights. Allison knew, even before she could see him clearly, that it was Martin, and her heart leaped with joy.

"It's him!" she cried out. "Father, that's Martin!"

Before Percival could reply to his daughter's shout of joy, she was running across the tarmac. She was in Martin's arms by the time he reached the bottom step.

Martin was surprised to see her, and even more shocked by the exuberance of her greeting. But he recovered quickly, and when she turned her lips up to his, she found him willing and eager to respond.

Martin was given a five-day leave to recover from his ordeal, and he and Allison went to Scarborough-on-the-Sea for a small holiday. They'd toured the ruins of Scarborough Castle, then had eaten in a small cafe with a terrace overlooking the North Sea, and now they were in a hotel room, listening to the sound of the surf.

"For a midwestern boy like me, there is nothing to compare with those sounds," Martin said. "Listen."

They were quiet for a while, as the sea outside serenaded them with hollow boomings, great splashing tumbles, long hissing whispers and resonant thunders. It was almost as if the sea were speaking to them, though with only half-heard voices, tantalizing, but not direct.

163

Allison and Martin had taken a room together, so there was no doubt in either of their minds where this relationship was heading. But when they were faced with the moment of truth, nervousness pushed that moment back, and now they waited hesitantly before they crossed the line of commitment.

"Martin," Allison finally said. "Tell me about your family."

Martin laughed. "There's not much to tell really."

"But there must be," Allison said. "Besides, it isn't fair that you should know so much about my family, and I know so little of yours."

"I told you that my father publishes a newspaper," Martin said. "What I didn't tell you was that he was also a college professor. He taught English at the college I attended, Standhope College. Since the war, though, he no longer teaches."

"What's the name of the newspaper?" Allison asked.

"The *Mount Eagle Crier,*" Martin said. "Mount Eagle is the name of my home town. It's in Illinois, downstate, right on the banks of the Mississippi River. It's really quite a pretty little town. I think you would like it."

"A pretty *little* town did you say? I thought everything in America was big. Bigger and better," Allison teased.

"Careful, your prejudices are showing," Martin

said. "I thought we had worked through all that and emerged better people."

"You're right, I'm sorry," Allison said, smiling at his censure. "Please, go on. Tell me everything."

"Well, my mother's name is Nancy," Martin said. "She's a typical middle-class American mother, I suppose. She's active in garden clubs and that sort of thing. Then there's Charlie. Charlie is the brains of the family."

"Who is Charlie?"

Martin laughed. "I like the way you say his name—with that accent of yours. I guess I must be the only person in the world who calls him 'Charlie.' Everyone else calls him Charles. Charlie is my brother, and he's younger than I am—at least in years. But in some ways he's like a hundred years old. Do you know what I mean? Charlie is the smartest person I've ever known, but he's not just book-smart, he's everywhere-smart. He understands things about people. It's funny . . . I'm older, and I'm the one who played football and basketball and baseball—you know, all the things that put you in the public eye. And yet I've always looked up to Charlie. Have you ever known anyone like that?"

"No," Allison said. "Not really. But I can readily understand that such people do exist. I'm certain he must be a wonderful person for you to have such a high regard for him, and I should like to meet him some day—though, given our circumstances, it probably wouldn't be too wise."

"Don't be so sure," Martin said. "If anyone in my family could understand this, it would be Charlie. He was the only one to stick by my sister."

"What do you mean?"

"On the night she graduated from high school, Dottie married her boyfriend Jim. She eloped."

"Eloped? How romantic!" Allison said.

"I suppose it was romantic," Martin said. "But it was also very foolish. Mom and Dad had wanted her to wait a while longer and not to rush into it. It broke their hearts when she left.

"Why did she do it?"

"She loved him, I guess," Martin said. He was silent for a moment then he spoke again, almost wistfully. "No, it's not just a guess. I *know* she loved him. He was in the army, and they wanted as much time together as they could have. He's overseas now, in Italy, I believe."

"How is their marriage?"

"Strong," Martin said. "And Charlie could see that, even before they were married. He stuck by them. I don't know, but I think he may have even helped them." Martin laughed. "My sister has a kid now—a little girl. I got to see her just before I left the States. Dottie is working with the Red Cross and she came out to the field before we took off. She's calling the little girl Holt. Well, that's it. That's the family."

"Not quite," Allison said. "There is still Yolinda."

"Yes," Martin said with a sigh. "There is still Yolinda."

"Aren't you going to tell me about her?" Allison asked.

"What's there to tell?" Martin asked. "She's my wife."

"There's more to it than that."

"We were high school and college sweethearts," Martin said. "I was the football hero, and she was the campus beauty queen. It seemed natural enough that we would get together. Her family and my family are friends, and that sort of added impetus to the inevitable. When I finished flight school, we were married. It was a big church wedding at St. Paul's Episcopal Church."

"Episcopal? Isn't that the Church of England?"

"It's what the Church of England became in America, yes," Martin said. "Anyway, we were married, and when I was posted to New York, Yolinda came along with me. Only she didn't like it. In fact, she hated it. All she did was complain about the living conditions."

Martin paused for a moment before continuing.

"There was Dottie living down in Alabama with Jim in a basement under the most horrendous conditions you could possibly imagine, while Yolinda and I actually had very nice accommodations furnished by the Army. And yet Yolinda hated it. Then, when she got pregnant, she blamed me and went back to Illinois.''

"Pregnant? Do you have a child?'' Allison asked.

Martin smiled. "It's a boy, and his name is Dennis. He's a real big kid. Charlie tells me he's big enough to be a tackle.''

"A tackle? I don't understand.''

"It's a position on a football team,'' Martin said. "Only the biggest and the meanest can play that position.''

Allison laughed. "And that's what you want for your son? For him to be the biggest and meanest?''

"Sure,'' Martin said easily.

"I can't believe that.''

Martin laughed at Allison's reaction. "You just don't understand the game of football,'' he said. "It's a rough sport. How do you think I hurt my knee?''

"What do you mean? I thought you hurt your knee in the war. I thought it was a flak wound.''

"I never said that,'' Martin said. "It was your idea that the injury was a war wound.''

"But you led me on,'' Allison protested. "You let me believe that.''

Martin laughed. "It was good for sympathy. If I had told you I hurt it playing football, do you think you would have been as concerned for me?''

"You tricked me, Martin Holt," Allison said. "I won't forgive you for playing on my sympathy."

Though her words were harsh, the look in her eyes and the smile on her face told Martin that he really had nothing to worry about.

"Martin, do you feel guilty?"

"Guilty?"

"About us, I mean?" Allison said. "Do you feel guilty about what we are doing? Do you feel adulterous?"

"Yes," Martin admitted. "Even though Yolinda isn't being faithful to me, I still feel guilty."

"How do you know she isn't being faithful?"

"I got a letter," Martin said. "In fact, that is why I was in London the day you met me. I had just received the letter, and I was going into town to get even."

"Get even?"

"You know . . . pick up a Piccadilly prostitute. But when I got into town I sort of lost my desire to get back at her, and I just looked for a place to sleep. That was how I met you, and we had so much fun that I forgot all about Yolinda. I don't even feel a sense of anger or betrayal toward her now. In fact, I feel sorry for her. The truth is, we probably shouldn't have married in the first place. She is obviously terribly unhappy, and she must feel trapped by circumstances. I'm sorry to be the cause of that unhappiness."

"Oh, Martin, how could anyone ever be un-

happy with you?'' Allison asked, then she gasped
and put her hand to her mouth. ''I'm sorry,'' she
said. ''I'm afraid I just spoke out of turn.''

Martin smiled as he reached for her and put his
arms around her.

''No,'' he said. ''That kind of comment is never
out of turn.''

Martin kissed her, then they separated, and Allison started toward her suitcase.

''The loo is just down the hall,'' she said. ''I
think I'll take a bath, if you don't mind.''

''No, I don't mind,'' Martin said. ''You go
right ahead. I'll just sit here and watch the waves
roll in.''

''Don't just sit there; start a fire in the fireplace,
why don't you? With the night air off the sea, it's
cool enough for one, don't you think?''

''I sure do,'' Martin said.

As Allison walked down the hall to the bathroom,
her head was spinning, and she felt a hollowness
in the pit of her stomach. She had never done
anything like this before. And yet here she was,
about to commit adultery. It wasn't a spontaneous,
spur-of-the-moment adultery, but a planned four-
day jaunt, with adultery its only purpose.

Allison may have felt a hollowness and a
spinning, but there were other sensations which
were far more dominating right now. She felt an
ache such as she had never before experienced,

and a warmth ran through her body, as if her blood had suddenly turned to hot tea.

She took great pains during her bath to make herself ready for Martin. She bathed in scented waters, and she softened her skin with oil. Then she combed her hair out and put on a negligee Elaine had loaned her.

"I guarantee you, ducks, the sight of you in this little number will turn stone to butter," Elaine had said.

When Allison returned to the room a few moments later, Martin was sitting on the sheepskin rug in front of the fire he had built. He turned to look at her, and he gasped, awed by the incredible picture of beauty she presented. Her hair hung loose and soft against her shoulders, and the fire made her eyes glow, as if lighted from within.

The negligee Allison was wearing was so sheer that she might as well have been wearing nothing at all. It had seemed so right when she was planning it, but now she felt a momentary sense of alarm. Perhaps she shouldn't have gone quite this far.

Allison looked at Martin's eyes, and they reflected an obvious appreciation of her body as he drank her in. His gaze lingered over the promising shadows at the junction of her thighs, then moved down her well-shaped legs to her bare feet.

"Perhaps a bit much, don't you think?" Allison asked nervously. "Maybe I should put something over me to—"

171

"No," Martin said quickly, interrupting her in mid-sentence. 'Don't you change one thing."

Allison stood there for a second longer, then he held his arms out toward her, and she went to him, grateful to be able to do something to interrupt the awkward moment.

She walked over to Martin, and sat beside him on the sheepskin rug. She went into his arms and they kissed, deeply this time, like lovers. The tenderness was still in their kiss, but it was overlaced with an intensity which had not been present before.

"Allison," Martin said softly, and his lips caressed her eyes and ears as lightly as the flutter of a butterfly's wing. "I think I've found what I have been looking for all these years."

"What is that?" Allison murmured, thrilling to his touch.

"I have found someone I truly love," Martin said. "Before I met you, I never really knew what love was. I love you, Allison. I love you more than I have ever loved anyone—more than I ever thought possible. I love you more than life itself. If I died tomorrow, I could die happily, knowing that, once, I knew love."

Allison put her arms around Martin's neck and pulled his lips down to hers. She could feel the texture of his lips as she kissed him, and her mouth opened hungrily on his, as if she could consume him.

The events seemed to unfold in a dizzying array

after that. At some point Martin must have removed his clothes, because she could feel his naked body against hers, though she didn't remember when it happened. Then the soft caress of the night air and the radiated heat from the crackling fire in the fireplace touched her skin and told her that she too was naked.

Just as Allison didn't remember Martin removing his clothes, she also couldn't recall taking off her negligee, nor could she recall the exact moment they moved to the bed. But here they were, with their naked bodies pressed together, lying in bed side by side.

Outside, the surf continued to pound, and in the fireplace the fire popped and cracked, and the noises seemed to blend together in a sensuous rhythm that was pounding with the intensity of kettle drums and matching the beats of her heart and the pulse of her blood. And as the exciting rhythm weaved its way through her body, Martin's hands and mouth and lips led her to the edge of ecstacy, brought her to a maddening precipice that beckoned her only onward.

Martin moved over her then, and as she felt his weight pressing against her, she opened herself to him and abandoned all thought but this headlong quest for sensual pleasure. She was lifted to fantastic peaks, felt a joy burst over her with the brilliance of a rocket's glare.

Then Martin began shuddering in pleasure too,

telling her that he had joined her in this maelstrom of sensation. Allison locked her arms behind his naked back to provide him with the cushion he needed to ride out his passion and desire.

Later, with the pleasant weight of Martin still on her and only the heavy breathing to tell of the experience just past, Allison closed her mind and her heart to any possible regrets. She intended to take what joy there was for her now, for she did not know what the future would bring.

9

"It's 'bout time you come around," Sergeant Morris whispered harshly. "I was beginnin' to think you'd found some other poor bloke what was in need of your attention and you'd forgot all about your boy Alex."

"Everyone in this hospital needs my attention," Midge replied.

"Yeah?" Morris said. "Well, do they need the same kind of attention you been providin' for me?"

"Why should it matter to you?" Midge asked. "You haven't been neglected in any way, have you?" Midge turned the sheet back, then lifted the hem of Sergeant Morris's nightshirt.

"I been waitin' for you," Morris said then, "as I believe you can tell by takin' a look at what I've got for you."

Midge looked at the erection thrusting obscenely up and gleaming at her with its purple head, winking at her with its one impatient eye and arresting her with a serpent's hypnotic power. She stared at it for a moment longer, then reached out and wrapped her long, cool fingers around it.

"Ah, yes," Morris said. "Yes, that's what I've been waitin' for. Go ahead, love, do your duty now."

Midge began working her fingers up and down, feeling its seductive smoothness and its terrible heat. She was repulsed by its ugliness, yet absorbed by the strange fascination it seemed to hold for her. She continued to manipulate the throbbing flesh until a series of muscle spasms caused it to erupt in spurts. She held it until the jerking subsided, then she began to clean it with a warm, damp cloth.

"You like it, don't you?" Morris said.

"What?"

"I used to think you come up here just to do this for me," Morris said. "But I been watchin' you. Behind these 'oles there's still eyes, 'n I been watchin' you. You like it."

"I . . . I'm glad I am able to help you," Midge said. "That is my purpose."

"No, miss, it's more'n that," Sergeant Morris

said knowingly. "You like doin' it, 'n me bein' like this just makes it easier for you, that's all."

"Good night, Sergeant Morris," Midge said, pulling the bedsheet back over him.

She left the ward. She walked quietly and quickly down the dark aisle between the beds, then stepped out into the hall, where she was surprised to find Dr. Thompson. He stood looking at her with a smug expression on his face.

"Teddy, what are you doing here?"

"Well, now, your *Ladyship*," Teddy said. "You've done your good deed for the night, have you?"

There was an unpleasant tone to his voice, a tone which frightened Midge.

"I . . . I don't know what you are talking about," she said.

Teddy chuckled. "I mean your little visit to Sergeant Morris, of course. How long has it been going on? Two weeks? Three?"

"You . . . you know?" Midge asked in a small voice.

"I didn't until tonight," Teddy said. "I must say, it is a sporting proposition you are offering poor old Alex. After all, you couldn't possibly derive much satisfaction from such a visit."

"I'm not looking for my own satisfaction," Midge said. "I just thought I might be of some service to Sergeant Morris, that's all."

"*Service* to Sergeant Morris?"

"Yes. I couldn't help but recall the conversation we had that night when you told me how the poor man was suffering."

"Ah yes, my lecture on sex and the male orgasm," Teddy said. "But obviously you didn't pay close attention. I said that as long as there was an alternative means of seminal emission, the spontaneous emissions would not begin. You are inhibiting that goal, Mrs. Waverly."

"I'm sorry," Midge said. She gestured helplessly. "I . . . I just couldn't let him lie in there night after night and suffer, couldn't bear to think of the agony he was going through—particularly as you were using me to contribute to that agony."

"And you decided to become the angel of his relief, is that it?"

"You might say so," Midge said.

Teddy shook his head and smiled a small, knowing smile.

"No, my dear lady," he finally said. "You might have convinced me if this had happened only once. But obviously you've gone back to him again and again. You can't convince me, and you can't convince yourself."

"I . . . I'm sure I don't know what you are talking about," Midge said.

"You know what I'm talking about," Teddy said. "Sergeant Morris was right, wasn't he? You *do* like it?

"Dr. Thompson," Midge gasped. "Were you *in* there?"

"I was just on the other side of the screen," Dr. Thompson said.

"You should have made your presence known, Doctor," Midge said.

"What? And spoil all the fun?"

"It was a most ungracious thing for you to do," Midge said.

Teddy put a hand on his crotch. "If you think *that* was ungracious of me, wait until you see what I have planned next."

"What are you talking about?" Midge asked in a trembling voice.

"There's an examining room in here," Teddy said, indicating the room with the jerk of his thumb. "You are going to go in there with me."

"Why should I go in there with you?"

"Let's just say that I have needs too," Teddy said. "Sergeant Morris isn't the only one."

Midge gasped. "No," she said. "I am not going in there."

"Oh? You disappoint me."

"I disappoint you? Did you really think I would? What kind of person do you think I am?"

"I think you are a person who would not like to be dismissed from staff for immorality," Teddy said.

"What are you talking about? What do you mean?"

"If you do not go into the examining room with me, I shall have you relieved of all your duties. And the reason I shall give is that I caught you visiting the patients at night in order that you might take indecent liberties."

"You wouldn't do that, would you?" Midge asked in a small, frightened voice.

"Oh, I would," Thompson said. "I most decidedly would." He stepped across the hall and opened the door to the examination room. "After you, your Ladyship."

Midge hesitated, then stepped through the door and into the center of the room. It was illuminated only by the bars of light which shone in through the overhead transom. Dr. Thompson turned on the red lights, and everything in the room began to glow in a soft ruby color.

"It's a nice effect, don't you think?" Teddy asked. He began unbuttoning his white coat, and Midge stood there, watching in stunned silence. "The other women I've brought in here seem to like it."

"You've been in here with others?"

"Yes," Teddy admitted. He smiled. "I do hope you aren't jealous."

"What you have done in here is no concern of mine," Midge said.

"Good, I'm glad we understand each other," Teddy said. "Now, get undressed quickly. We are both on duty, and we can't afford to be away too long."

"Dr. Thompson . . . Teddy . . . *please*," Midge begged. "Don't make me go through with this."

"It's really for your own good," Teddy said, as he continued to undess. "I have your best interest at heart."

"You have *my* best interest at heart? How can you say that?"

"You need to understand that there is more to a man than a penis."

"What?" Midge said. "What are you talking about?"

"Tell me, Midge, how is your relationship with your husband?"

"My relationship with my husband is none of your business," she said angrily.

"I am making it my business," Teddy said. He was totally nude now, and he stepped over to Midge and began undressing her. He did it clinically, as if she were a patient and he the doctor.

Midge didn't resist, but she didn't help either. She stood there quietly as Teddy unfastened the buttons of her blouse one by one, then stripped it off. He pushed her skirt down next, then took the hem of her slip and pulled it up over her head.

"Haven't you ever wondered why you have been so attracted to Sergeant Morris?" Teddy asked. The slip joined the rest of her clothes lying on the floor and shimmering in a pool of red. Teddy reached around behind her and unfastened her bra, then pulled it off. Her nipples tightened in the air and shone blood-red in the night light.

"Attracted to him? He . . . God help him, he is repulsive!" Midge said.

"Exactly my point," Teddy said. "He is a man without a face, without hands and, for now, without even the ability to walk. He has only one functioning organ, and that is his penis. Don't you understand yet, my dear? Sergeant Morris is no danger to you because Sergeant Morris doesn't exist. He is merely a support system for the penis that you need."

"No," Midge said. "No, that isn't true. You don't know what you are saying."

Teddy slid Midge's panties down to the floor, then stepped back to look at her. She was a woman of perfect proportions, and in this light she looked as if she were the artistic creation of a master sculptor who had chosen red marble as his medium.

"Show me it isn't true," Teddy said. "Show me you can deal with a whole man."

Midge looked into Teddy's face. She tried hard to fix her gaze there, to avoid looking anywhere else, but she couldn't keep her eyes away. They were pulled, as if by some unseen force, down across his body until they were fixed upon that part of him which held such a strange and terrible power over her. Then, moving as if he were in a trance, Midge dropped to her knees and reached for it.

"No!" Teddy said sharply, pushing her away. Midge looked up at him in confusion. "But I thought you wanted—"

"I want you to respond to *me*," he interrupted. "To the *man*."

Teddy reached down and pulled Midge up by the shoulders. He led her to the examining table. He helped her up on it, then raised the stirrups and put her feet in them so that her legs were spread apart. He walked to the end of the table and stepped up between her legs. Midge looked down her body at the man who loomed over her. His eyes gleamed red, not only from the lights of the room, but, it seemed, from the very fires of hell itself. As he thrust into her, Midge closed her eyes to blot out everything but the onrushing sensation of pleasure she felt.

Midge stood in the bathroom and watched the water run into the tub. The tub was nearly full, but she made no effort to turn off the tap. The sound of the running water massaged her mind and soothed her troubled spirits. Only when the water was in danger of spilling over did she finally reach down and shut it off. She stepped into the tub, then lay back and looked down at herself. Her breasts floated up from her body, and the tendrils of hair at the junction of her legs moved in the water like seaweed, as if to welcome someone to the rapture of the deep.

That would be good, Midge thought. If only she could slip away, slip deep into the sea and, wrapped in the comfortable coils of seaweed, be held forever in sleep. Suicide. She should commit suicide. She couldn't live with this evil which had visited itself upon her.

She took a razor from the corner of the tub. She opened it, put the razor's edge to her wrist. She felt the sharpness of the blade. For a moment she tensed. Just a slight sting, that's all it would be. A slight sting, then she would know peace.

She closed her eyes and waited, but the sting didn't come. She opened her eyes and looked at the razor, as if she could will it to do her bidding, but the razor remained fixed in her hand. No matter how hard she willed it, she could not make her hand push the blade into her veins.

With a sob of frustration, Midge threw the razor across the bathroom floor.

So she couldn't commit suicide by cutting her wrist . . . . Well, there was more than one way to get the job done. She would find another way, and it would be slow and painful.

10

Karen Hornsby lay in a bed still heavy with the musk of lovemaking and looked at her husband. He was dressed now, and he stood silently at the window of their sixth-floor flat, gazing out over the rooftops of London.

It was a lovely flat, complete with a terrace, where they had eaten their breakfast this morning. Sometimes Karen felt a little guilty about having such a nice apartment, for all over London small, dingy rooms were renting at exorbitant rates. But Karen's husband Phillip owned this entire building, and though he had generously donated several suites to the British government for their wartime use, he had reserved the choicest suite for himself.

Despite the fact that Phillip had reserved himself such a nice flat, he seldom got to enjoy it. As a Flight Lieutenant in the R.A.F. he had to spend most of his time at the air base and managed only one or two nights freedom per week. Even at that he and Karen were lucky, and they knew and appreciated their good fortune. They were both aware of the fact that many husbands and wives faced a wartime separation of years.

Karen was the youngest of the three Cairns-Whiteacre girls. She had volunteered as a member of the skywatch, a duty less demanding than the jobs held down by her two sisters and one which allowed her to take advantage of Phillip's free time.

Karen was neither as beautiful as Midge nor as self-assured as Allison, although she was a very pretty girl. Unlike her sisters, Karen was quiet and withdrawn, and she sometimes found herself envying them. Neither Midge or Allison ever seemed to fear anything, and they were both so beautiful and outgoing, with a vivacity which Karen felt she could never hope to match. Compared to them, she considered herself a little mouse, but she loved her sisters, and had always looked up to them and basked in their radiance.

What Karen had not been able to see in herself, Phillip Hornsby had seen immediately. She was a girl with a quiet, but deep passion and, though unexpressed, a thirst for life which was unquenchable.

Phillip had perceived this the first time he met her, and he had instantly appreciated Karen's beauty, even past the dazzling charm of her sisters. When they were married, some among Phillip's friends were totally unable to see what Phillip saw in Karen, and wondered silently if perhaps Phillip had married the title rather than the girl. Even those who most dubiously questioned the marriage, however, were made believers when they saw the two together. The bond of love between Phillip and Karen seemed to strengthen with each passing day.

"Phil, are you all right?" Karen asked, as he continued to stare out the window.

Phil turned to look at Karen. The sheet had slipped down so that one small breast, flattened into her chest by her position, was visible. The nipple, still tightly drawn from the recent lovemaking, was all that gave evidence to the fact that the gentle swell of flesh was a mature woman's breast.

"I'm fine," Phil said finally, smiling at his wife.

"You seem so pensive."

"Do I? I'm sorry. I was just thinking, I suppose."

"What were you thinking about?"

"About us," Phil answered. "About how lucky we are to have each other, especially now when so few can be together."

"I know," Karen said. She sat up in bed and brushed her hair back with a careless toss of her hand. Now both breasts were visible; though small, they were exquisitely formed.

Phil walked back to the bed and sat on the edge of it. "That's why we really have no complaint, no matter what the fates may deal us," he said. He spoke the words casually, but Karen caught the impact of it at once.

"Phil! Oh no, you are going out tonight, aren't you?"

"You know I can't tell you that, darling," Phil said. He put his hand on her cheek and moved his fingers lightly on her skin. She reached up and put her own hand on his.

"You don't have to tell me," Karen said. "I know you are going out."

Karen put her arms around him then, and she felt the rough texture of his uniform against her bare nipples. Her body was still sensitized from the recent lovemaking, and she still held the warm wetness of his semen in her. A small tingling sensation, a pleasure almost like a secondary orgasm, tremored through her as she leaned into him.

"Don't worry, darling," Karen said. "You'll come back safely, I know it. I don't know how I know, but I know that we'll be together when this war is over.''

Phil gave a small, nervous laugh. "Don't we have our roles reversed here? Aren't I supposed to be the one to tell you to keep a stiff upper lip and all that?"

"You can tell me if you want," Karen said, smiling at him.

"Keep a stiff upper lip," Phil said, chucking her playfully under the chin.

"I'll do that, providing you keep something stiff for me," Karen said.

"What's that?"

Karen smiled seductively, and realizing what she was talking about, Phil laughed aloud.

"My, aren't you the brazen one, though? It just proves what they say: Still waters do run deep."

"You don't have to be going yet, do you?" Karen asked, lying back invitingly on the bed.

Phil began unbuttoning his tunic. "No," he said. "I don't suppose I have to be back right this minute."

"Hello, E for Edward. This is Whitefish. Come in, please."

"Whitefish, this is E for Edward," Phil replied. "Go ahead."

"E for Edward, you may test your guns now."

"Roger, Whitefish," Phil answered. He switched

his radio to intercom, then called his crew. "Pilot to gunners, test-fire your guns."

Phil's instructions were answered with the hammering of machine guns, and Phil could see the brightly colored tracer rounds spitting out into the cold black vault of night sky and forming long golden strands of jewels before him.

The target tonight was Hamburg. It was to be the fourth attack on Hamburg in as many days, two attacks having been made by the Americans, bombing by day, and this, the second attack by the British, bombing by night.

This was the coordinated attack promised by the British and American air commanders, and the operation, code-named *Gomorrah*, was planned to last for two weeks.

Phil had not been on the first night attack. On that night the British had utilized a new weapon: the H2S radar device, a method of painting an electronic picture of the ground below so that the blackest night could be penetrated. For the first time, too, they'd used 'Window,' an amazingly simple means of foiling German defensive radar. Window consisted of nearly one hundred million strips of aluminum foil which were dumped by the approaching bombers as they entered the German radar range. Each strip would register a blip, so that to the Germans it would appear as if millions of airplanes were attacking instead of the six hundred which actually carried out the raid.

190

On the first night of the raid British bombers delivered three thousand tons of incendiary bombs. The following day United States B-17s attacked Hamburg, and the next day the Americans bombed again. Now it was night, and the British were coming back for their second raid with a massive attack force consisting of 722 airplanes.

"Lieutenant?" the top turret gunner called down. "Lieutenant Hornsby, what is that ahead, sir? Do you see it?"

"Yes," Phil answered. "I see it."

The gunner had called Phil's attention to a bright glow, a false dawn on the horizon ahead of them.

"My God, look at that," the bombardier said. "It's like looking into the bowels of hell."

"It's Hamburg," Phil said. "Still burning."

The bombers continued toward Hamburg. When they were close enough to see not just the hellish glow but the very fires themselves, the signal was sent to cross the aiming point and deliver the bombs. Phil tried to close his mind to what was going on beneath him and to concentrate only on flying.

When Phil dropped his bombs, he helped to create a firestorm which caused death and destruction of a magnitude never before known. Old fires joined new fires, and as the air was heated, it rushed upward and caused cooler air to fill the vacuum thus created. The ocean of fire moved such a volume of air that an artificial hurricane moving at two hundred miles per hour turned the streets of Hamburg into blast furnaces. Cars and trees and buildings were sucked into the center of the fire by the in-rushing winds, and so it was that the fire continued to burn by supplying itself with fuel. Temperatures soared over two thousand degrees, and the heat sucked the oxygen out of shelters and incinerated those trapped inside.

Phil's plane dropped its bombs, then rejoined the bomber stream heading back to the home base. Fighter activity had been extremely light, because the British had once again used Window with devastating effectiveness.

"Well, that was a piece of cake, eh?" the bombardier called up to Phil. "We bloody well ought to be ashamed to take our paychecks this month after—"

A sudden explosion cut the bombardier's comment off, and when the flash of light dimmed, Phil saw that the entire nose section of his plane had been shot away by an anti-aircraft shell. The bombardier who had been ashamed to receive his pay for such an easy mission was no more. Phil didn't know if he had been torn to pieces by the exploding shell or simply blasted out of the plane. There was no way to tell, as the bombardier's station no longer existed.

Phil didn't have long to ponder the situation, for the blast had also severed the control lines. He was no longer flying an airplane, but riding inside a hunk of uncontrolled—and uncontrollable—flaming cinder.

"Pilot to crew, pilot to crew, bail out!" he called. "Bail out! I have no control over this aircraft."

Phil hit the bail-out warning bell, and even over the roar of wind and propellers he could hear its ring. As he looked around and saw two of his men leave the ship, the great bomber nosed down and started into a spin. Phil released his seat belt, pulled himself into a ball and plunged through the hole in what had been the nose of the ship.

Phil kept the tuck position he had assumed for bail-out as long as he could. He fell like a cannonball, and that was what he wanted to do because he knew that the aircraft, even though crashing, would fall more slowly due to the wind resistance. Finally, when he thought he had put a safe distance between himself and the airplane, he pulled the ripcord.

The shock of the opening chute jerked into his shoulders so hard that he felt as if his arms were going to be pulled out of their sockets. It was the best feeling he had ever experienced, for now he knew that his fall toward the ground had been checked.

Phil had only had a moment to savor that feeling when he heard a roaring sound above him. He looked up and saw that the airplane he had just exited was coming right at him! He closed his eyes and mouthed a quick prayer, then felt the propwash of the still functioning engines as the plane roared by, and then, mercifully, he was above the plane as it continued its fall down.

The plane crashed and exploded just below him, and the fire from the burning plane illuminated a plowed field. Phil hadn't realized he was that close to the ground; almost before he knew it, he hit.

Phil rolled with the landing shock, felt a bruising blow, but noted, almost subconsciously, that he had not hurt an ankle or a leg. That would have made a getaway impossible. Now, at least, he had a chance.

As soon as he was able to stand, Phil collapsed the chute which was billowing forth from the surface wing. He ran upwind of it, then gathered it and took it to the burning airplane, where he threw it into the flames. He had the idea that if the chute wasn't discovered, he would have a better chance, for the Germans would surely think he perished in the crash.

Phil wondered about the rest of his crew. Was anyone still in the plane?

The fire was too hot to allow a good look, but Phil tried to get close anyway. He saw one gunner's station, but when he squatted down to try to look inside, no matter how hard he tried, he could see nothing.

Suddenly Phil heard some shouts, and then he realized that the burning airplane was acting just like a beacon and leading Germans right to him. He ran out of the bubble of light and jumped down into a ditch which ran close by. Bent over he ran through the ditch until he reached a small thicket. He climbed out of the ditch and slipped into the trees. Only then did he stop to catch his breath, and when he did, he turned to look back toward the plane.

There were half a dozen people, perhaps more, gathered around the plane. From this distance he couldn't tell if they were farmers or soldiers, but they all appeared to have guns. He didn't really care who they were. He only knew that they were Germans, and that he would have to avoid them at all costs if he was to make good his escape.

Phil moved quietly through the trees until he came to the edge of a dirt road which appeared to be deserted. He moved out onto it, because it was easier to walk on the road and he figured he could make better time. He walked on for some time, until, suddenly, he heard German voices. He dove from the road into the weeds alongside.

Phil lay there, barely daring to breathe, as two German soldiers came walking down the road from the direction in which he'd been heading. He had not seen them earlier because of a slight rise in the road, and he knew that if they hadn't been talking, he would have run right into them.

After the soldiers passed, Phil moved back out onto the road, but this time he vowed to be more alert to his surroundings. He had taken a foolish chance before, and he would not make that mistake again.

Just before sun-up Phil spotted a haystack, and he decided that it would be a good place to spend the day. He crawled into the haystack, pulled the hay around him and slept. When he woke, it was late afternoon and the sun had already turned red in its descent. Smoke and haze from the still burning fires of Hamburg created a spectacularly beautiful sunset. Phil felt a twinge of guilt over the fact that so many people had died to create that sunset.

Phil was ravenously hungry and thirsty. The thirst bothered him more than the hunger, so he decided to take a chance and come out, even before dark, to see if he could find some water.

Phil found food before he found water. He discovered a small garden and dug up several potatoes. They were not very large yet, only about half the size of a lemon, but to him they were as welcome as a rack of lamb.

There was something else useful in the garden. There was a scarecrow, and it was dressed in a man's pants and shirt. Phil took the scarecrow's clothing and put it on over his flying suit. He was afraid to take off his uniform, because out of military dress he could be shot as a spy. He could cover his uniform with these clothes, though, and that might provide him with some protection.

A short distance from the garden, Phil found a

water pump. He began pumping the handle desperately, and finally he was rewarded by a cool stream of water. With one hand cupped under the nozzle, he pumped with the other and drank until he had his fill. He wished he had a water bottle so that he could take some with him.

"What are you doing?" a woman suddenly asked in German.

Phil could speak a little German, as he'd visited Germany a few times before the war. But he spoke it so poorly and with such an accent that he knew he would give himself away the minute he opened his mouth.

"Answer me!" she demanded again. "Tell me what you are doing or I shall call the authorities!"

"*Wasser bitte*," Phil answered, hoping that in those two words he wouldn't be discovered.

"Are you with the workers who are digging the ditch?" the woman asked.

Phil didn't understand the entire question, but he did understand that she was asking him if he was a worker.

"*Ja*," he answered.

"The next time one of you wants water, you have your leader come and request it of me, do you understand? I'll not have just everyone tramping through my garden, drinking my water, stealing my things. Your leader must request for you."

"*Ja*" Phil said. He nodded, then turned to go.

"Where did you get the pants and shirt?" the

woman asked before he had taken more than a step, and Phil knew that she had recognized the clothes as having come from her scarecrow. Suddenly she grabbed for the shirt.

As Phil twisted out of her grasp, the buttons of the shirt popped open and his uniform was clearly visible beneath.

The woman screamed.

"Englander! Englander!"

Phil turned and began to run. He ran for the corner of the house, but when he turned the corner, he found himself in the middle of a camping squad of German soldiers. The soldiers had heard the woman's warning cry and were ready for him. One of them shot a burst of automatic weapon fire into the air and called for Phil to halt. Phil stopped and put his hands in the air.

The squad sergeant, the one who had fired the gun, walked up to Phil and grinned at him.

"So," he said, speaking English, "we have captured an English flier, have we? This will mean an extra beer ration for each of us. I must thank you for coming down in our zone."

"Kill him," one of the other soldiers said, also speaking in English. "He is one of the bastards who bombed Hamburg. Kill him!"

"Is that right?" the sergeant asked. "Did you bomb Hamburg?"

"No," Phil lied. "I fly weather reconnaissance. I was in an unarmed plane when I was shot down."

The sergeant laughed. "Such an inglorious mission to have you be shot down," he ridiculed. He turned to the one who wanted Phil killed. "Why should we kill him? He is such a little fish."

"Kill him anyway. The bombers cannot bomb if the weather is not good."

"But this one does not make the weather, he only flies around and looks at it," the sergeant explained with a laugh. "Alive, he is worth an extra beer ration. Dead, he is worth nothing. I do not intend to kill him."

"I say we should."

"And I say we won't, and *I* am the sergeant," the sergeant said, now growing a little angry with the recalcitrant member of his squad. "I shall give the orders around here."

"*Jawohl*," the soldier who had wanted to kill Phil mumbled in contrite reply.

For the first time in his life, Phil was glad for the strict German discipline.

"I'm glad you like beer," Phil said to the sergeant, trying to joke with him. He thought he might be able to ensure friendlier treatment if he could get the German into a conversation.

"All Germans like beer," the sergeant answered.

"We British are a bit more partial to ale," Phil said. "But the Americans like beer."

"I don't like American beer," the sergeant said. He smiled broadly. "For three years, I lived in

Milwaukee. That is in America—have you heard of the place?''

"Yes," Phil said.

"Milwaukee is a very nice town," the sergeant said. "There are many Germans there. That is where I learned to speak English."

"You speak English very well," Phil said.

"Thank you."

Phil was accomplishing just what he wanted to. If the German regarded him as a person rather than as a prisoner, he would be less inclined to shoot him.

"Tell me, friend, what is going to happen to me now?" Phil asked.

"Don't worry," the sergeant said. "Do as you are told and you will be well treated. We Germans treat our prisoners of war very well. You will get soup and black bread every day." He laughed. "I wish always that our army could eat so well."

The sergeant had sent one of his men into the village, and now the man returned with two police officers in a car. The police officer got out, issued a receipt to the sergeant, then motioned for Phil to get into the car.

"This is for our beer," the sergeant said, smiling as he held up the paper.

"Enjoy," Phil said sarcastically.

Phil was handcuffed, then shoved roughly into the back seat of the police car, and both policemen got into the front seat. Neither of them said a word during the drive, despite Phil's attempts to engage them in a conversation.

When they reached the prisoner of war camp, Phil was handed over to the guards. For the first time, he was searched.

The guards confiscated the potatoes he had stolen, then took his ring, watch and compass. After he was photographed and fingerprinted, he was taken out into the prison compound.

Phil looked around at the place which was to be his home for a while.

The compound consisted of several long, low wooden buildings or barracks. The structures were built of unpainted, weathered wood and stood in neat rows across the compound grounds. In the center was what appeared to be an assembly area, and enclosing the compound was a high chain-link and barbed-wire fence. Guard towers, complete with searchlights and machine guns, were placed strategically around the fence. Phil could tell at a glance that every square inch of the compound was under the observation of at least two of the towers.

Phil followed the guards across the compound yard. He saw several prisoners moving around quietly, some working in small gardens, others standing together in private conversation. They looked at him with interest, but not with undue curiosity.

"You will be assigned your billet by your senior

201

officer," one of the guards said. He smiled. "It is a concession we have allowed the prisoners. In return for giving your senior officer the privilege of making assignments, we have your word that you will not attempt to escape."

Phil looked at the guard, but he said nothing. A British officer came over toward him.

"That's quite all right, Sergeant, I'll handle it from here," the British officer said. He was a colonel, and Phil could remember having seen him somewhere, though he couldn't place him for the moment.

"Very well, Colonel," the German sergeant said. "Treat him gently, as he is still in shock from being captured," he added, and laughed at his own joke.

The British colonel waited until the Germans were gone before he spoke.

"You don't know what shock is until you discover that you Boche are losing the war," he said under his breath. Then he looked at Phil and smiled as he extended his hand warmly. "Right. Well, you're Phil Hornsby, aren't you, old man? I'm Colonel John Dawes. I believe we've met before."

"I must admit I've been trying to place you," Phil said.

"I was General Beckoncourte's adjutant for a while," Colonel Dawes said.

"Oh yes, please forgive me for not placing you more quickly," Phil said.

"No matter," Colonel Dawes said. "As the adjutant, it was my job to remain invisible, but efficient. Now I'll fill you in on things around here."

"I don't intend to be here very long," Phil said.

"Well, that's the right attitude," Colonel Dawes said. "In fact, I hope none of us are here much longer."

"How long have you been here?"

"Oh, I'm the senior officer both by rank and by longevity. I was shot down in a Wellington back in the summer of '40. I doubt if any of the old Wimpys are even flying anymore, what with the Lancasters and Stirlings handling all the bombing chores nowadays."

"You've been here since 1940?" Phil asked, shocked by the revelation.

"That I have, lad," Colonel Dawes said. "That I have."

"Good lord, is escape *that* difficult?" Phil asked.

"Escape?" Colonel Dawes laughed. "Dear me, lad, I've not even *tried* to escape."

"You haven't even tried, Colonel? It's the duty of every prisoner of war to try to escape."

"You'll discover that we have our own interpretation of duty here," Colonel Dawes said. "I interpret my duty to remain here, to ride herd over my boys. I've never even thought of trying to escape."

"Colonel Dawes, I don't know what your interpretation of duty is, nor do I care. I intend to escape from this place just as soon as I can.''

"You will attempt your escape, Lieutenant," Colonel Dawes said in a crisp military voice, "if, and when, the escape committee approves of your plan. I will *not* have the lives of others jeopardized by any bungled escape attempts on your part. Is that clearly understood?''

Phil ran his hand through his hair and looked at the shorter, balding Colonel. Finally, he sighed.

"Very well, Colonel—I'll play by your rules insofar as I will allow your escape committee to approve of my plans. But I'm telling you right now, I have no intention of sitting out the remainder of the war in this prison.''

Colonel Dawes looked at Phil, and for a long moment their gazes locked each other in a battle of wills.

"Then I think we shall get on nicely," Colonel Dawes said.

"Fine. In the meantime, where shall I bunk?''

"In barracks five," Colonel Dawes said. "This one, right here.''

Phil looked at the barracks. "Very well. If you don't mind, Colonel, I think I shall go in and take a nap now. I've had very little sleep for the last few days.''

"Sleep as long as you wish," Colonel Dawes said.

Colonel Dawes watched Phil go into the barracks,

and he was still looking toward the barracks when another prisoner approached.

"A new fellow?"

"Yes," Colonel Dawes said.

"What do you think of him?"

"I think he's going to be a runner," Colonel Dawes said. "We are going to be hard-pressed to keep him in line with everyone else. He's anxious."

"Yes," the prisoner said. "But then, aren't we all?"

11

Captain Gregory Waverly was endur-
ing a nightmare. Of the sixty men who had
embarked on the long-range penetration behind
Japanese lines, fewer than forty remained. Many
of those who remained were suffering from dysen-
tery, and all were plagued by the relentless on-
slaught of jungle insects and other pests.

Food and water had become a problem as well,
and the Waverly Raiders, as the men had boldly
called themselves when they'd embarked, were
now dependent upon the very jungle which plagued
them for their sustenance.

The company had been in the jungle for forty-five days now, and they had enjoyed some success in disrupting Japanese communication and supply lines, but the cost of sustaining the operation was growing daily. Greg had established a base camp along the banks of a wild river, chosen because it was impossible for a surprise Japanese attack to be launched at this site. He chose it also because here, at least, was a supply of water.

Greg was sitting with his back to a tree and burning leeches off his body with a lighted cigarette. He was listening to a discourse by his second-in-command, Hollis Winfield.

"Listen, Greg, what do you think? Monkey stew can't be all that bad, can it? I mean, the bloody natives eat it all the time." Hollis was not only Greg's second-in-command; he was also his best friend.

"I haven't forbade anyone from eating the blighters," Greg said. "I simply said that I didn't want to try it myself."

"I really think you should," Hollis said. Hollis, who was as naked as Greg, walked over to his commander and turned to allow him to burn the leeches from his back.

"Give me one good reason why I should," Greg replied.

"Well, we are running short of rations, aren't we? And if you don't do it, many of the men won't. Some of them will die if they go much longer without something substantial to eat."

"But a *monkey*, Hollis. Isn't that a little like eating . . . I don't know . . . they are so human-like that it is almost like cannibalism."

"Not at all, old man," Hollis said. "There are no dangerous psychological problems caused by eating monkeys. There could be from cannibalism, but I must remind you that even cannibalism has been resorted to in certain extreme cases."

"Well, I certainly hope you don't propose *that* action," Greg said. He burned the last leech from Hollis's back, then turned his own.

"Of course not," Hollis said. "That simply isn't necessary. We have an ample source of food without resorting to that extreme. Provided, of course, you take advantage of it. What do you say? A little monkey stew, simmered slowly in its own juices, flavored with a bit of wild pepper, jungle onion, bamboo shoots, mustard and palm root. Sounds good, doesn't it?"

Greg laughed. "Has anyone ever suggested that you might try writing copy for a restaurant somewhere? I've not seen bills of fare in the finest New Delhi establishments make their menu sound so good."

"Then you will try it?" Hollis asked with all the enthusiasm of a new bride trying a dish on her husband.

Greg sighed. "Well, you've sold it so well, how could I possibly refuse? Who knows? I may get to like it so well that it'll replace pudding for a Christmas treat.''

"You won't be sorry, old man, I promise you," Hollis replied. "In fact, I'll cook it myself. Now, all I've got to do is shoot one of the screaming little devils, and we're all set.''

"Hollis, if you don't mind . . .'' Greg started.

"Yes, old man? You have a special request?''

"I do," Greg said.

"You name it, and I'll take care of it.''

"I don't want to see the bloody thing until it is already simmering in the pot,'' Greg said. "And I don't want any descriptions of killing it either.''

Hollis laughed. "Right you are. After all, would the head chef at Maxim's let you in his kitchen before he served dinner? Not at all, I can tell you. You just relax. I'll call you when it is already simmering in the pot, just as you like.''

"All right," Greg said. He slipped his uniform back on, then checked the chamber of his weapon. "I'd better lead a patrol out anyway. We wouldn't want the Nips to crash our little dinner party, now would we?''

"Not a bit of it," Hollis said. "Oh, by the way.'' He mimicked an Indian batboy, getting the accent down perfectly. "Any idea when I might expect sahib for dinner?''

"I should be back in about three hours,'' Greg promised. He smiled wryly. "If I'm not, start without me.''

210

"Yes, sahib," Hollis said, holding his hands together under his chin and bowing.

Greg laughed at the antics of his exec, then sauntered through the camp with his weapon slung over his shoulder. Four men stood up to join him, even though he didn't say a word. Despite the hardships the company had endured, the morale of the men was still high, and nowhere was that better evidenced than by the fact that volunteers never had to be called for. When someone saw that a job needed doing, they did it without being asked.

Greg and his patrol moved swiftly and silently through the jungle for nearly an hour before they heard Japanese voices. Greg held up his hand and the patrol stopped. Silently he signalled for the others to get into place, and they slipped behind cover on either side of the trail. Greg waited until the Japanese patrol was completely by them, then gave the signal. His men stepped out onto the trail behind the Japanese and opened fire. Greg and all his men were armed with automatic weapons, whereas the Japanese were armed with rifles which had to be manually operated to rechamber a round after each shot. The Japanese outnumbered the British, but they were badly out-gunned and managed only a weak and ineffective response.

Greg felt the recoil of the automatic weapon against his shoulder, and as the gun sprayed out the spent cartridges, hot little specks of gunpowder flew back in his face. His eyes and nose burning from the spent gas and his ears ringing from the sound of the gunfire, he held the trigger down and hosed his fire into the group of Japanese soldiers.

The British fire cut down palm leaves and splattered bark from the trees, but much of it found its target, and after a short, but furious fusillade, the last Japanese soldier fell.

"See if any of them are carrying food," Greg said.

Two of Greg's men went up to check the fallen soldiers and searched quickly and efficiently through the uniforms and rucksacks of the Japanese.

Greg looked down at one of the dead Japanese soldiers. His billfold had slipped out and flipped open. There was a picture of a Japanese girl dressed in a kimono and holding an umbrella open before her. In the back was a *tori* gate. She was smiling shyly, as if embarrassed by the whole thing.

Greg swore, and kicked the billfold so that it sailed several feet before disappearing in the thick foliage. What was he doing? He knew better than that. He could not let himself think of the enemy as people. If he thought of them as real people with girl friends, wives, mothers, fathers, sisters and brothers, he could go crazy. But then, what does it matter, he thought. The whole bloody world is crazy anyway. Only crazy people would kill other people who carried pictures of loved ones in their wallets.

One of Greg's men came back and shook his head slowly.

"Captain, these poor beggars are as bad off as we are. There's not a thing on any of them. Did you find anything on this one?"

Greg looked at the owner of the billfold he had just kicked.

"Nothing," he said. "They say misery loves company, but I wish the Nips had a little food. It would at least make killing them more profitable."

"Think we ought to hide the bodies, Captain?"

"No," Greg said. "Look for maps or anything else of military significance, then let's get on back. Lieutenant Winfield has a little surprise cooked up for us, I think."

"Is your steak too rare?" Colonel Kluever asked Midge. Colonel Kluever was an American officer on the combined staff of Invasion Planning and Operations. He had heard about Midge through a friend, and was told that she could be a lot of fun on a date. He had asked her out, and now they were eating dinner at the American Senior Officers' Open Mess at the Savoy in London.

"No," Midge replied. "It's just fine, thank you."

Midge sliced into her thick cut of meat and watched as the juices flowed. The meat was brown on the outside, pink just beneath the surface and quite red in the middle. It was smothered in mushrooms, and a large baked potato was to one side of it, fluffy white with a yellow pat of butter forming golden rivulets down its sides.

"I suppose there are some who would criticize us for taking up shipping space with such things as steak and wine," Colonel Kluever went on. He had been explaining his theory of psychological philosophy in geopolitics. "But it is very important psychologically that we do just that. Well, you can understand why readily enough can't you?"

Colonel Kluever didn't wait for an answer. "You see," he continued with his discourse, "the very fact that we *can* do it shows the great strength of the United States. I mean, after all, here we are, building up our forces for the largest invasion in the history of mankind . . . Why, we have tanks, planes, guns and ammunition—all the combined firepower of all the armies in history couldn't equal what we have here—and yet, in the Senior Officers' Open Mess, we can enjoy a steak as fine as any you could find in the entire state of Texas."

Colonel Kluever topped off his statement with a large bite of meat. He chewed it with relish and closed his eyes in appreciation, then took a swallow of California Burgundy.

"Yes, sir," he said. "This is turning out to be a fine war—a very fine war indeed, when one is in position to take advantage of it. And we, my dear, are in just such a position." He toasted her with his glass. "Let us enjoy."

"Yes," Midge said, touching her glass to his. "I agree. By all means, we should enjoy."

After the dinner there was dancing, but during the middle of the dance the music suddenly stopped and the wail of hundreds of sirens could be heard all over the city.

"Ladies and gentlemen, the coastwatchers have spotted a wave of V-1 bombs headed for London," someone announced over the microphone at the bandstand.

There was a quick and nervous reaction from those in the club.

"If you would, please remain calm," the announcer went on. "Proceed quickly, but calmly to the nearest air-raid shelters. We have at least ten more minutes before the first bombs arrive."

"Drat," Colonel Kluever said. "Just when the party was getting good, the damned Germans have to do something like this."

"That is most inconvenient of the Germans," Midge said sarcastically. She knew as soon as she said it, though, that her sarcasm was lost on the Colonel. She knew it because she had been sarcastic all night long and it had all been equally lost on him.

Midge hated Colonel Kluever. She had never met him before tonight, and though she would sleep with him tonight, she would never see him again. She hated him because he represented everything that she hated about herself.

Midge knew that it wasn't fair to blame Colonel Kluever for what she was going to do. It wasn't fair to blame him any more than it was fair to blame Teddy Thompson or Sergeant Alexander Morris for showing her what kind of person she really was.

There had been dozens of men since Teddy Thompson. Dozens of men had warmed her bed before this overweight, bushy-eyebrowed, pompous ass she was with tonight, and dozens more would warm it after this night.

The scenario was always the same: an elegant dinner, a gay party, and then a night of sex, as Midge proceeded down her own special path of self-destruction.

Midge was no longer working as a volunteer nurse. She no longer saw her mother, or her father, or either of her sisters. In fact, she consciously avoided them, and didn't even call Karen when she learned that Phil had been taken prisoner by the Germans.

It wasn't only her own family she avoided. She refused to return any calls from any of Greg's family, and though no one had heard from Greg in over four months, she didn't even offer Greg's family the comfort of sharing their concern.

Outside, the sirens ceased their wail, and for several seconds there was a sound of approaching engines. Searchlights stabbed into the sky. In the distance anti-aircraft guns began firing, and big overhead winks of lights flared like lightning flashes as the shells exploded.

"It's not a very large raid at all," Midge observed. "Nothing at all like the raids during the Battle of Britain. This is just a nuisance raid, I suppose."

"Shouldn't we go to a shelter?" Kluever asked, and Midge was secretly pleased that he was so frightened.

"The greatest danger will be from our own anti-aircraft shells falling back on us," Midge explained. "We can avoid them just by getting inside somewhere."

"Where?" Kluever asked. "You tell me where and we'll go. I think we should get inside, I really do."

"Anywhere is all right," Midge said. "How about your flat?"

"My flat? Do you think it's safe in my flat?"

Midge reached up and unbuttoned Colonel Kluever's collar button.

"That all depends," she said.

"On what?"

"On what you fear most," Midge said. "If you are afraid of the air raid, you'll be safe enough. But if you are afraid of me . . ." she let the statement hang.

Colonel Kluever was obviously torn between

two emotions. He was clearly intrigued by the sexual overtones of this incredibly beautiful creature with him, but he was also moved by the more basic instinct of survival. He was terrified by the air raid.

"Listen," he said, "couldn't we just go to the shelter now? Just until the all-clear is sounded, and then we could go to my apartment and—"

"No!" Midge said sharply. "It's now or never, dearie. Take your pick."

Kluever looked at Midge, saw her in the reflected glare of the hundreds of searchlights which ringed the city. A tiny line of perspiration beads popped out on his upper lip.

"Okay," he said finally, with a sigh. "Okay, you win. But, lady, damn if I don't think we are both crazy."

Midge gave a low, throaty laugh, then followed him back into the Savoy.

The elevators were not working during the air raid, so they had to take the stairs up to his room on the sixth floor. They could hear the muffled crumps as the guns fired, the more distant cracks of the shells exploding high over head and then an occasional heavy boom as one of the V-1s crashed somewhere in the city. Kluever kept looking around nervously and jumping with each explosion as they ascended the stairway.

"This is the floor," Kluever said, his voice quavering, when they finally reached the sixth.

Midge, amused by his fear, smiled as she followed him down the hallway to his room. With shaking hands Kluever unlocked the door, then pushed it open. Midge stepped inside. Kleuver followed her and turned on the light.

There was a loud air-raid whistle from the street below.

"Turn off that bloody light, you idiot! You want to bring the bombs down on us?"

Kluever quickly turned the light off again. "I wasn't thinking," he said. "I didn't realize what I was doing."

Midge laughed the same low, throaty laugh again. "The V-1s are pilotless planes," she said. "The lights really don't make any difference. I think the wardens just keep them off to make people believe that they are doing something, when actually there is nothing they can do. Whenever the engine stops . . ."

As she was speaking, they heard the pulsing jet of one of the bombs clearly approaching them. Kluever took in a gasping breath and held it, then looked up toward the ceiling, as if he could see through it to the lethal bomb high overhead. The engine didn't stop, and the bomb buzzed on beyond them.

"See? Nothing to worry about. It went right on by," Midge said. "Now, take off your clothes, won't you?"

"I . . . This is preposterous," Colonel Kluever

said. "Can you imagine what people would say if we were killed and found up here like this?"

"What difference would it make?" Midge asked. "We would certainly be beyond caring, wouldn't we?"

Midge began taking off her clothes, and a moment later she was standing in the reflected glow from the window. A bomb or a returning anti-aircraft shell had started a fire somewhere, and though it was too far away to actually see the flames from the hotel, some of the orange glow mixed with the silver of the reflected searchlight glare. Midge's nude body was well enough lighted to be clearly visible.

Kluever gasped as he looked at her. She was perfect in every detail, from the ember-tipped, conical breasts to the flat stomach to the flaring thighs and tapered legs. The orange glow of the fire reflected off the light-colored bush of hair at the junction of her legs and made it appear like a spade of glowing coals.

"My God," Kluever breathed reverently. "I have never seen anyone as beautiful as you. You must be Satan's own handmaiden. What are you doing here anyway? How could anyone as beautiful as you wind up here? With me?"

"Maybe it's just your lucky day," Midge said. She walked over and stretched out on the bed, where she waited for him as he quickly stripped out of his clothes. Outside, the guns continued their crashing thunder, and nearby, close enough that they could hear the tinkling of glass, a bomb exploded. By now, however, Kluever was beyond concern.

The Colonel walked over to the bed and got down on one knee. He looked at Midge, almost as if in worshipful homage to her, then leaned over to kiss her breasts. The touch of his tongue on her nipples sent shudders of pleasure rippling through her.

Kluever got into bed with her, and in a moment Midge felt his weight upon her. For an instant she felt the same sense of disgust and anger with herself that she always felt, and she wished for a moment she could call back what she had started. She had only wanted to punish him and punish herself. She hadn't intended to let things get this far. How *had* they gotten this far? Why hadn't she used the razor on herself when she'd had the chance? This path of self-destruction was truly the slowest and the most painful. She didn't deserve this. Dear god, she didn't deserve this.

And then the doubts and self-recriminations began to disappear, to be pushed aside by the rising tide of pleasure which coursed through her body. She lay beneath him, and silent, unprotesting, she rode the cresting waves of pleasure which were beginning to sweep over her.

Midge opened herself to him and began to use him. She was sharing nothing with him, but rather was taking from him all she could for only her own pleasure, and when she groaned, it was not to let him know of her rapture, but merely to reinforce her own quest.

She thought of the crippled and maimed soldier, Sergeant Alexander Morris, and she became one with him, a pitiful creature alone, a creature using and taking and needing until the white heat of orgasm burst over her.

12

Gineral Sir Percival Cairns-Whiteacre
had recommended early in 1943 that the overall
commander of the upcoming invasion be an American. His recommendation was not a popular one
with his fellow British generals. Nearly everyone
had assumed that the position would go either to
General Morgan, who had done much of the pre-
liminary planning, or to General Brooke, the Chief
of the Imperial General Staff. A few even sus-
pected that General Montgomery, who was considered England's most capable combat commander,
would get the nod.

By the end of 1943, however, it gradually became clear to even the staunchest Anglophiles that it would be sensible to name an American as the supreme commander for the invasion. In December of 1943, the supreme commander for the invasion, which was now code-named *Overlord,* was appointed by President Roosevelt. His choice was General Dwight David Eisenhower.

General Eisenhower was an excellent choice, Percival liked to point out to those who grumbled over the fact.

"After all," Percival told the others. "He did spend two years in the Mediterranean proving that the English Tommy and the G.I. Joe could function well as a team."

Percival also liked to point to a statement General Eisenhower made in reply to a rather bitter attack on the propriety of his being appointed to the position.

"Perhaps any number of generals, American and British, would have been a better selection," Eisenhower said. "But as long as this duty has been placed upon me by Great Britain and the United States, I have no recourse except to do my very best to perform it adequately."

"It's an unbeatable combination," Percival said to all who would listen, "British technology and experience combined with American industrial might and manpower."

Part of the British technology Percival referred to was the development of man-made harbors.

Winston Churchill himself had originally proposed man-made harbors for a planned invasion of Flanders during World War I. Like the tank, also a Churchill innovation, the harbors were brought into fruition in time for use in war a generation after the idea had been born.

More than two hundred steel and concrete pilings were developed, each as big as a five-story building. They were designed to be towed into position, then sunk off shore. Once positioned, they would create an artificial harbor of protected water for the unloading of invasion ships.

Percival had been an early convert to the idea, and because he was also an early supporter of the appointment of an American, he was selected to brief General Eisenhower on the plan. Thus it was that on the 20th of May, 1944, Percival met General Eisenhower for the very first time.

Percival didn't know the exact date of the invasion, but he knew that it must be near because the briefing documents were classified as *Top Secret* and *Most Urgent* and were labeled *Harbors, final briefing*.

"I want to tell you a few things about Ike before you meet with him, Percy," General Morgan said. "He is a most deceptive man."

"Deceptive? You mean he is duplicitous?"

"No," I didn't mean deceptive in a negative sense," General Morgan said. "It's just that he is not a man prone to vain affectations. He has a terribly engaging grin, but a rather low-key personality that makes you wonder, at first, how he ever made it so far. Your first impression of him is likely to be that he is a very *nice* man—too nice, in fact, to have any business conducting the affairs of war.''

"I take it, however, that there is a man beyond the first impression?'' Percival asked.

"Oh, definitely,'' General Morgan said. "Just when you have been lulled into thinking he doesn't quite have the picture, you suddenly discover that not only does he see what you see, but also much much more. It can be most disconcerting—rather like playing a poker game to one deuce showing and finding that there are three more deuces down.''

Percival laughed. "I think I will avoid playing poker with him.''

"An excellent idea. He happens to be an outstanding poker player.''

Percival stood up and picked up the case with the harbor briefing material. "Well, I shall keep my wits about me when dealing with General Eisenhower, and if I am lucky, I will still have them when the conference is concluded.''

General Morgan laughed as he started toward the door with Percival.

"Oh, by the way, Percy, have you heard anything from either of your sons-in-law? One of them is in a German prisoner-of-war camp, isn't he?''

"Yes," Percival said. "The Red Cross delivered a letter from him shortly before Christmas. He is, or was at that time at least, in good health. I must confess that we have heard little from Gregory."

"That's Captain Waverly? He's in the Indian Army, isn't he?"

"Yes, in the Burma theater."

General Morgan clucked his tongue. "Those chaps had an amazingly posh show before the war, but I must say they are paying for it now. It has been as rough a go for them as it has been for any of our lads anywhere. Well, I do wish the best of luck to both of them. You have three daughters, don't you? The third one is not married I believe."

"That's Allison," Percival said. "There is an American chap she is seeing on a regular basis now. Just doing her bit for Anglo-American relations, you know."

General Morgan laughed. "I think quite a few of our English girls are giving their all to that cause. If your daughter is serious about this American fellow, I hope he is in some nice, safe staff job somewhere and not an aviator."

"I'm afraid he *is* an aviator," Percival said. "He is a B-17 pilot."

"Oh dear. The American insistence upon daylight bombing is thinning their ranks terribly. I hope her young man is one of the lucky ones."

*   *   *

227

After Percival left General Morgan's headquarters, he proceeded directly to General Eisenhower's SHAEF, or *Supreme Headquarters of the Allied Expeditionary Force*. SHAEF was headquartered in a large camp at Bushy Park by the Thames River in Middlesex, but Eisenhower's personal headquarters were located in Telegraph House, a large, elegant house very near the park. Percival had known the house for years and had always admired it. He thought it was particularly suitable as the headquarters for the supreme commander.

"General Eisenhower will see you now, General Whiteacre," a lieutenant colonel announced. Percival thanked him, then walked into the room which had once been a dining room and was now General Eisenhower's office. The General was on the phone as Percival entered.

"I don't care how important he is," Eisenhower was saying. "He is not indispensable. One of the biggest problems we face is in maintaining the best personal relationship possible between us and the British. If one of my staff called an English officer a son-of-a-bitch, then I don't need him. Send him out to the field and move his deputy up to replace him."

Eisenhower hung up the phone and looked up at Percival. He smiled, and extended his hand in greeting.

"I guess you overheard," Eisenhower said. "I'm

sorry that some of my men can't seem to keep a civil tongue.''

''General, if I may be so bold,'' Percival said, ''perhaps you over-reacted. We English used to be disturbed by the constant American references to another's genealogical background, but we have come to realize that you chaps throw around the phrase 'son-of-a-bitch' with no more thought than we use for the word . . . chaps. What I mean to say is, we are not really offended by it anymore, and I'm certain that the English officer involved would have no wish to see the American officer so severely punished for his poor choice of words.''

''Perhaps so, General,'' Eisenhower said. ''But, you see, the American officer called the English officer a *Limey* son-of-a-bitch. And that I won't have.''

''I must confess, General Eisenhower, to an admiration for your perception of subtleties,'' Percival said, laughing.

Eisenhower joined Percival in laughter, then invited him to sit down. A moment later Percival was served tea, and he realized that in that, too, Eisenhower had scored favorably, for most American generals automatically served coffee and thus catered more to their own taste than to that of their visitors.

''Let's hear what's happening with the artificial harbors,'' Eisenhower said, by way of inviting Percival to begin his briefing.

"I think you will be quite pleasantly surprised," Percival said, and he opened his briefcase.

"General Whiteacre," said Eisenhower at the conclusion, "I'm convinced that this idea for artificial harbors will be one of the most important innovations, if not *the* most important, in the entire operation. You and the others are to be congratulated on a job well done."

"General, your words are too kind," Percival said.

Eisenhower chuckled. "I've been told that the Prime Minister himself had the original idea for the harbors. Other than being a brilliant politician, an outstanding orator, an inspired tactician, an inventor, painter, writer and historian, your Mister Churchill really doesn't have much going for him, does he?"

"I beg your pardon, General?" Percival replied. Then, realizing that Eisenhower was joking, he laughed. "Oh, yes, I see what you mean. Winnie does like to keep his hand in things."

"We Americans are quite proud of the fact that Mr. Churchill is one-half American," Eisenhower said.

"Indeed, I think it is a fact that England is equally proud of. After all, it does cement our relationship, doesn't it?"

"Yes, it does," Eisenhower agreed. "General,

I would like to make a personal request, if you are agreeable to it.''

"I am at your service," Percival answered.

"I know you are very busy with your current assignment, but as most of the English real estate has now been taken up by us, I wonder if I could persuade you to join the combined staff in planning for the invasion itself? I would be particularly interested in your following up on the harbor installation so as to ensure the steady and uninterrupted flow of supplies, once we are lodged on the continent.''

"General, are you serious?" Percival asked, his eyes shining in excitement. "I . . . I can think of no task I would rather undertake. You would have my undying gratitude if you were to use me in such a capacity.''

"Fine, fine," Eisenhower said. "I'll speak to General Brooke about it. I'm certain all the arrangements can be made.''

"Thank you, General," Percival said again, pumping Eisenhower's hand vigorously. "I'll be looking forward to the assignment. I'm extremely grateful for the opportunity.''

"It will be good to have you on the team," Eisenhower said, as he showed Percival out of his office.

Percival left Telegraph House in a most ebullient mood. The idea that he would actually get to take part in the largest invasion in military history was thrilling to him.

As he slipped into the back seat of his car, Percival got another surprise. The driver wasn't the same young lady who had brought him here, but his own daughter.

"Allison? What a pleasant surprise!" Percival said. "How did this happen?"

"I saw the duty board when I came on," Allison explained. "When I saw that Jean had driven you to Telegraph House, I asked to trade with her. I hope you don't mind."

"Mind? What are you talking about? I think it is wonderful," Percival said. "Why would you think I would mind?"

"Well, I did it for a personal reason, actually," Allison said.

Percival laughed. "I should think a daughter wanting to see her father is personal enough."

"I mean another personal reason," Allison said. "I have something I want to ask you."

"What is it?"

"I would like to invite Martin out to Ingersall this weekend. Would that be all right, do you think?"

"Of course, it would be all right," Percival said. "In fact, I've often wondered why you haven't invited the young man out. I know that the war has played havoc with convention, but it needn't destroy every custom. I think a father and mother should still be allowed to meet the young man their daughter is seeing on a regular basis. You are seeing him regularly, aren't you?"

"Yes," Allison said. "I've been seeing him as often as his duty will allow."

"Then what is it? Why haven't you had him out before now? Oh, I think I know. Is it because of the title? Most Americans are a little intimidated by titles, I believe."

"That is partly the reason," Allison said. "But there is another reason as well. Father . . ." Allison paused, then took a deep breath. "Martin is not free," she said. "He is married."

Percival let out a long, concerned sigh. "Oh," he said. "Oh my, that does make a difference, doesn't it?"

"Not to me," Allison said. "I love him, Father. I love him very much, and what's more, he loves me. We want to get married."

"You want to get married, do you? Well, see here, won't that be a little awkward? I mean, after all, there is the problem of a spare wife now, isn't there?"

"Martin is going to divorce Yolinda as soon as he returns to the States," Allison explained. "He doesn't want a long-distance, wartime divorce, and I don't either. Somehow that seems so sordid, and I don't want anything about our relationship to be considered sordid."

"I see," Percival said.

"He also has a son, Father," Allison said. "His name is Dennis."

"A child as well as a wife?" Percival said.

"Allison, do you feel no compunction about breaking up a man's home and family?"

"I'm not breaking up his family," Allison insisted. "If one wanted to get technical about it, Yolinda left Martin before he ever came over here. Martin told me they were together at an air base in New York and she left him. In fact, Martin has never even seen his son."

"Darling, you are a grown woman now, and I can no more decide how you should live your life than I can decide how Midge should live hers. Midge seems to have come to her own accord with things, and her conduct has deeply saddened me, but I have said nothing to her. Nor will I."

Allison also knew about Midge. Once she had even carried two American officers in her car while they compared notes about her sister. She had been stung by the revelation, but she said nothing to Midge or to anyone else in her family. She was a little surprised to learn that her father already knew of the situation.

"I hope you aren't comparing me to Midge," Allison said.

"And I hope you aren't making a value judgement on Midge," Percival replied. "After all, we don't know what she has been through or what she is going through. Do you think your own situation is any different?"

"Yes," Allison said, and her eyes filled with tears. "I'm not married, and Midge is."

"Perhaps not, but then your young man is married," Percival said.

"But Midge is . . ." Allison was about to say that Midge was going from man to man, whereas she had only one man, but she held her tongue. It wouldn't help her position any to degrade Midge further.

Percival leaned across the seat and touched Allison tenderly on the shoulder.

"I'm sorry, darling, I know there is a difference," he said. "And I know that these things do occur. If you'll remember, I was one of the few people to support David in his decision to abdicate his throne to marry the American, Wallis Simpson. Surely, if a king can fall in love with a married woman and garner my support, my own daughter deserves no less. If you love him, I shan't stand in the way. And if you wish to bring him to Ingersall, then, by all means, do so. Your young man will be most welcome."

"Oh, thank you, Father," Allison said. "Thank you very much. You are a dear, dear man."

"Yes, that's what Ike thinks too," Percival said. "He has just asked me to join the combined operations and planning staff. It seems I'm to play rather a major role in the invasion."

"Oh, Father, what wonderful news! How proud you must feel!" Allison said.

"Yes, I am, rather," Percival said, scarcely able to contain how he did feel. "By the way, when did you say your young man would be coming?''

"This weekend," Allison said.. "He and I both have the weekend free, and I wanted to spend it with you and Mother."

"I'll look forward to seeing him," Percival said.

"And Mother?"

Percival chuckled. "Oh, I learned a long time ago that it is useless to try and guess your mother's reactions. She's quite unpredictable, you know. But I expect there will be no difficulty with her. She's an exceptionally fine woman, with attributes that not even her own daughters realize."

"Mother has a mysterious quality to her," Allison said. "I don't know what it is, but sometimes she seems quite preoccupied. I think she may be taking her job as head of the Ladies' Hospital Brigade too seriously. It worries me."

"Your mother has a lot on her mind now, Allison—more than you can ever know. But don't worry about her. She is capable and strong, and she will be fine."

"But she can't stay any longer," Lady Anne was saying. "The Germans have broken her cover. They know that Kani Ben-Ahr is Carmen."

"She insists upon staying, Lady Anne, and if she is so insistent, there is really nothing we can do," Mark said. Then, after a short pause, he added, "except be thankful."

236

"Be *thankful?* Be thankful that she is virtually committing suicide by staying?"

"We can be thankful that we have a woman of such courage," Mark said. "Lady Anne, you are too closely involved with Carmen to see things clearly. But she is quite right, you know. This close to the invasion, there is no way we could get anyone else in there. If we pulled her out now, we would not have time to replace her."

"And if she is killed? Who will we have on station then?" Lady Anne asked.

"We will at least have her until she is killed or captured," Mark said.

"Yes," Lady Anne replied. "We will at least have her until then."

13

When Martin first drove through the gates of the estate, it took his breath away. Ingersall Hall was so awe-inspiring as to be overpowering, and he stopped his jeep for just a moment so he could look at it.

Allison saw the jeep from her room, and she hurried downstairs so she could greet him the moment he arrived. She had been trying to convince Martin to visit Ingersall Hall for nearly a year, but until now he had steadfastly refused. He was intimidated by the titles, true enough, but mostly he was embarrassed to be a married man paying court to a woman in the bosom of her own family. Allison had finally persuaded him to come, and, now, it was so important that nothing go wrong.

It was a beautiful day for the visit. The weather had cooperated to make it a warm May day. Allison wore white shorts and a bright red blouse in celebration of the occasion.

The butler beat Allison to the door, and he had answered Martin's ring. But Allison was downstairs by the time Martin came inside.

Martin gazed up at the high ceilings, vaulted and decorated with paintings, looked around at the polished mahogany, the leaded glass windows and the massive furniture.

"It's a little different from your apartment, isn't it?" he said as she greeted him.

"Be it ever so humble," Allison replied. She was always a little self-conscious about the grandeur of her family home, and she was trying to pass it off lightly.

"All this house for just two people?"

"Of course, there are the servants," Allison said.

"Of course," Martin said. "And how many servants might there be at Ingersall Hall?"

"Just twelve now, but before the war there were thirty."

"It must be difficult, getting by with only twelve servants," Martin teased.

"After all, there is a war on, you know, and we must make some sacrifice," Allison replied, laughing. There was a time when she would have perceived a barb in Martin's tease, and she would have been hurt and reacted sharply. Now she was so comfortable with him that she was able to take such things in stride.

"Oh," Allison said. "Here's Father."

Martin shook hands with General Cairns-Whiteacre, who looked very distinguished and proper in his uniform and with his greying hair and moustache.

Percival looked Martin over. So, this was the American pilot his daughter was head over heels in love with. Percival had met him briefly the night he had been rescued and flown back to England, but this was his first opportunity to examine the young man critically.

He was a good-looking fellow, Percival thought. And he was certainly more than a mere garrison soldier enjoying the hospitality of England. Percival knew about Martin's flying record. He knew that the young man had been through hell, and he warmed to him immediately.

"Well, you've not seen Ingersall Hall before now, have you?" Percival asked.

"No, sir," Martin replied. He smiled. "I have read about it, though. I did my homework before I came out here."

"You *read* about it? My word, where would you have read about Ingersall Hall?"

"I have a book," Martin said. "It's a pamphlet,

really, put out by the War Office Printing Department. It's called the *American Officers' Guide to English Peerage, 1944*. It told about the house and the family.''

"I see," Percival said. "See here, did it tell *everything* about the family? Even our darkest secrets?''

Martin laughed. ''I know all about the rakehell Henry Alton Whiteacre, and how Arthur Cairns' claim to be the bastard son caused the name to be hyphenated.''

Percival laughed heartily. ''I say, you *do* know all our darkest secrets, don't you? Well, come along, I'll point out the grounds to you. But be careful, one never knows what skeletons might turn up in such a place.''

Martin laughed with him, and the two left the house with an anxious Allison looking on—anxious because she so wanted her father and her lover to get on.

''My great-great-grandfather put in this garden,'' Percival said, pointing to one section of shrubs, trees and bushes. ''Let's see, you had a fellow running around in America about that time by the name of George Washington, I believe.''

''It must be wonderful to be able to walk around and see the roots of your family from so many years ago,'' Martin said.

''I suppose it is, in a way,'' Percival said. ''But on the other hand, I have always greatly admired the Americans' wonderful sense of freedom and movement. You are not bound by your roots as we are.''

They walked on for a while longer, with Percival showing Martin other aspects of the estate. Finally, Percival cleared his throat, as if about to broach a subject of the greatest delicacy.

''I know about the, uh, domestic problem you have,'' he said. ''I'm not giving my approval, you understand. But human beings being human beings, I realize that such things often occur. I'll leave that up to you and Allison.''

''I appreciate your understanding, sir,'' Martin said. ''I can only promise you that I will never do anything to hurt your daughter.''

''Don't make promises you might not be able to keep, Martin,'' the General said. ''I only want you to do what you know is right . . . whatever that may turn out to be.''

''Yes, sir,'' Martin said.

''Well, we have a custom here,'' Percival said then. ''I get to show all our first-time visitors the grounds and garden, but Lady Anne reserves the right to show the house. So I suppose I had better take you back inside for the next part of the tour. I do hope you don't mind.''

''I don't mind at all, sir. In fact, I am finding it all very fascinating.''

''Good, I won't worry about boring you then. To some, I know this would all be rather stodgy.''

Lady Anne was waiting for them when they returned to the house, and she began her tour immediately. Taking Martin from room to room, she showed him ballrooms where Kings had danced, a desk Benjamin Franklin had used and an inkwell which, legend said, had been used by William Shakespeare. She also pointed out paintings of long-dead ancestors.

"Ah, so this is the old rapscallion himself," Martin said, as he stood in front of an oversized portrait of Henry Alton Whiteacre. Henry wore a Van Dyke beard and a large lace collar over a blue velvet waistcoat. He was holding a sword, and glaring out of the portrait with piercing blue eyes.

"Yes, this is the black sheep of the family," Lady Anne said, laughing good-naturedly.

Lady Anne showed Martin the bedroom he would use. It was as large as the entire upstairs portion of his family home back in Mount Eagle, Illinois, and Martin had always considered his house large. There was a tremendous fireplace on one side of the room, which was further furnished with a sofa and chairs as well as several massive chests and trunks. But clearly the most dominating feature of the room was the huge four-poster canopied bed.

"Disraeli slept in that bed," Lady Anne said.

There was a knock on the door, and Martin and Lady Anne looked around. Allison stood there, smiling at them.

"Are you and father going to monopolize him all the time, or will I have a chance to visit with him?" she asked. "After all, he is *my* guest."

"Of course he is, dear," Lady Anne said. "But he is such a charming young man that you can't really blame us for keeping him to ourselves for so long." She looked at Martin. "I do hope you will forgive us."

"Oh, but I enjoyed it," Martin insisted. "I truly enjoyed every moment of the tour."

"You are too kind," Lady Anne said. "But I am certain you would much prefer my daughter's company."

"He had better," Allison teased. "Do come with me now, Martin. I want to show you the lake."

"You have a lake, too?"

"Yes," Allison said. "I think it is the loveliest part of the entire estate, and I specifically told Father to save it for me to show."

Martin thanked Lady Anne and left with Allison to see the lake.

"This used to be the gamekeeper's cottage," Allison said as they approached a small building on the far side of the lake. "But we don't have a gamekeeper anymore, so no one uses it."

"It's very pretty," Martin said. "It would make a nice retreat."

"This is my favorite place on the entire estate,"

Allison said as they entered. She walked over to the bed, then turned around with a smile on her lips and her arms outstretched. "Come here, let me demonstrate this bed for you."

"Did Distaeli sleep here too?" Martin asked, grinning.

"No. But then sleeping is not exactly what I had in mind," Allison said, and she began to remove her clothes.

Martin walked over to her. "Turn around," he said. "Let me help you with your bra."

Allison turned around and Martin looked at the delightfully smooth skin of her back. He undid the bra and she moved her shoulders forward to let it fall. Martin reached around her, cupped her breasts in his hands and felt the tightening nipples with his fingers.

Allison turned her head back toward him, and kissing her open mouth, he took her tongue into his. Martin pushed her down to the bed gently, then moved onto it with her. Her eager hands soon divested Martin of his clothes, then she pulled him over her and guided him into her.

They made love fully and completely then, until a burst of wet warmth filled her and made them as one.

14

The Americans landed on Utah and Omaha Beach at 0630 hours in the morning of June 6, 1944. They were on the beaches for one full hour before the British, who hit the beaches of Gold, Juno and Sword at 0730. The difference in times was dictated by the different conditions the invaders faced.

The Americans chose 0630 because the tide would be at its lowest ebb and the underwater invasion obstacles would be exposed. The British chose 0730 both to ensure a longer pre-invasion bombardment and to enable the landing craft to ride in with the high tide which would place the men higher on the beach. The British also had another problem, one the Americans didn't have to face: a German Panzer Division.

Initially, the British had an easier time of it. The Germans had depended upon their Panzer Division to help defend the beaches to the north. To the south, without panzers, they depended upon strengthened fortifications, and they attempted to stop the Americans before they could come ashore. They were almost successful, and the American casualties for the first landing wave were extremely high.

General Sir Percival Cairns-Whiteacre was going to go in with the first wave of British troops to hit the beaches. He had justified his presence by convincing General Montgomery that it was imperative he be on the beaches as early as possible in order to expedite the placement of the artificial harbors. It was his own idea as he wanted to be part of the invasion force, and he didn't discuss it with anyone except Montgomery, with whom he passed it off as if he were acting under orders from General Morgan. Montgomery was occupied with so many last minute details that he couldn't take the time to check on Percival's story, which was just what Percival had hoped for.

Now Percival stood on the deck of the ship in the pre-dawn darkness, looking at the other men who had been shuffled up to their 'station' while waiting for the word to go over. They had been brought up at 0100, and many of the men, including Percival himself, had not slept a wink the entire night.

Percival wasn't sleepy, though, for his adrenalin was flowing too freely for that. He imagined that most of the others were just as excited as he was.

Suddenly, the heavens were lit with brilliant flashes, and Percival saw streaks of light speeding through the night, heading toward the shoreline. A moment after the light, the roar of explosions reached his ears.

"There they go, mates," an unseen soldier called from amidst those who were standing patiently on their station. "The Navy boys are givin' 'em what-for. I don't imagine there'll be much left by the time we get ashore."

"Oh, there'll be a bit of a show left for us, don't you worry about that," another voice said, and there was a nervous laughter.

The naval ships continued with their bombardment, and the sky all around them took on the illusion of a terrible thunderstorm, complete with brilliant flashes and stomach-shaking roars. Each time one of the navy ships would unleash a salvo, Percival could see the silhouette of the hundreds of ships which lay quietly at anchor off the Normandy coast.

"General Whiteacre? General Whiteacre? Has anyone seen General Whiteacre?"

"I'm right here, Lieutenant," Percival called out.

A young, terribly young, infantry officer stepped up to Percival. Good lord, Percival thought, this boy can't be going to war. But the awful truth was that a million others just like him, just as young and just as boyish, were waiting to engage in a life-and-death struggle which would determine the future of the world itself.

"General, I'm Lieutenant Collins, sir. I understand you will be going ashore with the first assault wave."

"Yes," Percival said.

"Fine, sir. You've been assigned to my boat. Have you practiced climbing down the nets, General?"

"No," Percival said. "But what can there be to it? You just climb down them, don't you?"

The young officer smiled.

"No, sir. There's a bit more to it than that, I'm afraid. If you don't mind, sir, may I give you a bit of instruction?"

"By all means, Lieutenant," Percival said.

"Here," Collins said, stepping over to a hatch bulkhead where a cargo net was being stored. He pulled out the net. "You can see that the net is composed of a series of squares formed by crossing ropes. Your feet go on the horizontal ropes, but your hands must grip the vertical ropes, like this."

250

"Why is that?"

"That's to keep your hands from being stepped on by the fellow above you," Collins explained.

Percival smiled. "I must admit that does make sense," he said.

"When you first go over the side, keep the upper part of your body leaning in toward the ship. Push out with your feet. If the upper part of your body should lean outward and your feet come in, you may find yourself parallel with the sea and you will have to hang on for dear life. Remember: the upper part of your body in."

"All right," Percival said.

"Be very methodical as you climb down. Remember that the ship is rolling. You may take a step and find there is no step there. Most of your weight should be borne by your hands. Your hands are for support, your feet for transportation. Don't look up, and don't look down. If you look up, the upper part of your body will swing out. If you look down, you can become disoriented. Now, and this is very important, when you get to the bottom of the netting, there will be net holders, men assigned to keeping the net away from the side of the ship. They will tell you when to disengage. You must disengage the moment they tell you, for with the rolling of the ship and the boat the last step can sometimes be as much as ten feet. Don't go before they give you the word, and don't hesitate once they have given you the word."

"Thanks, Lieutenant," Percival said. "I didn't realize it would be so complicated. I appreciate your advice."

"General, I wish I had known beforehand you were going to go ashore with us. I would have scheduled a practice for you."

Percival smiled. "I'll practice on my way down the net," he said.

"Now all troops to their disembarking stations, now all troops to their disembarking stations," a metallic voice said over a loud-speaker, and there was a general shuffling movement among the men who had been standing on deck for the last several minutes.

"First serial, into the boats, that is, the first serial, into the boats."

"Over here, General," Collins said, leading Percival to his place.

Percival watched as the men began climbing over the nets. One of the men slipped just as he was going over. He let out a startled scream, which was cut off sharply as he hit the deck of the boat below.

"What happened?" someone shouted.

"Did you see that?"

"Who was it?"

There was a rush to the railing. The loud-speaker ordered the men back to their proper places.

"He broke his back," someone said a moment later, and as the stretcher, suspended from a cargo winch, brought the hapless man back up, the others resumed their loading.

When Percival went over, Collins was right by his side, solicitous for his safety. He was glad for the young officer's dedication, and thankful when, at last, he was standing in the boat and waiting for the others.

Finally, the boats pulled away from the ships, then started circling while waiting for the waves to form. The circling may have been the most difficult part, if only because many of the men became so desperately seasick. Percival didn't throw up, but his stomach was pretty unsettled by the time the boat operator gunned the engine and pointed the boat toward the shore.

After everything else, the actual landing was somewhat anti-climactic. The portion of beach Percival landed on was relatively unchallenged, though he could tell from the gunfire and the explosions that many others weren't so fortunate. He moved off the beach with the advancing forces, then took up a position near the division headquarters to wait for the lines to stabilize.

By the next day, while the dead from the invasion were being gathered for return to England, phase two—the logistics phase—was well under way. It was Percival's responsibility to make certain that the follow-up to the initial invasion went smoothly. That meant additional men and supplies.

On the afternoon of the second day, a convoy of

old, dilapidated ships arrived. These were part of the artificial harbor which was to be constructed. They were carefully moved to the pre-selected location, then sunk. After the ships were sunk, piers were laid across their anchored hulls to provide a way of off-loading vehicles and bulky cargo which called for more stable conditions than open beach could provide.

Battle operations called for twenty-five divisions to be landed over the next twenty days, and the pier had a schedule it would have to maintain if the job was to be accomplished.

Percival had carefully worked out the schedule and promised General Eisenhower that he would be able to supply the army with everything it needed to sustain operations. Percival promised to handle 6,000 tons per day by D-day plus 5; 9,000 tons by D-day plus 12; and 12,000 tons by D-day plus 18.

Percival met his quota, and by the tenth day had already handled 183,000 tons of supplies and had landed 81,000 vehicles. Half a million men were put ashore.

"Do you know what Churchill is calling this?" General Eisenhower said to Percival, as he congratulated him on the logistical operation of the artificial harbors. "He is calling this majestic, and indeed it is. Our invasion is now secure, General Whiteacre, and it is due in no small part to your efforts."

"Thank you, General," Percival said, greatly warmed by Eisenhower's words.

"But let me tell you this," Eisenhower said, and now the tone of his voice changed to that of one who was scolding. "If I ever hear of you pulling another dumb stunt like the one you pulled when you went ashore with the first wave, I'll send you back to England."

"I'm sorry," Percival said. "It was just something I wanted to do."

Eisenhower looked at him for a moment longer, then flashed his infectious smile at him.

"Well, Percy, I can't really blame you," Ike said. "I believe I would have done the same thing if I thought I could have gotten away with it. At any rate, you did a fine job, and every soldier who has plenty of food and ammunition has you to thank for it."

Paris was in shambles. Much of the garrison which had held Paris captive had been moved out of the city to meet the advancing Allies. The lucky ones, and Ernst Goethe was among that group, were going back to Germany to help man the Siegfried line, the impregnable wall at the German border. It would, if all else failed, turn back the Americans and the British.

Only the SS was staying. The dreaded SS, those arrogant merchants of death dressed in black and silver and commanding the best of all Germany had to offer, were taking out their frustrations on the population of Paris. Goethe had never liked the SS in the first place, and since Kani Ben-Ahr had turned out to be an English spy, he liked them even less.

The SS had learned quickly of Goethe's friendship with Kani. He had tried to explain that she was only a neighbor, a girl who happened to live in the same apartment building as he.

"After all, I didn't choose that building," he had told them. "I was assigned that billet. I didn't choose my neighbors, they just happened to be there. And the Ben-Ahr girl was an exceptionally beautiful girl. Who can blame me for being friendly to her?"

Two weeks after that interrogation, Goethe was in a minor traffic accident. There wasn't really much to it. The truck which hit his car was driven by a private, a young man who was quite upset when he found that he had run into an automobile driven by a major.

Goethe put the soldier's mind at ease and sent him on his way. There was very little damage done, and Goethe had a strong dislike for paperwork. Then, after the soldier left, Goethe made a startling discovery. There, on the floorboard of his car, was a radio transmitter! It must have been wedged in under the dashboard, only to be dislodged by the accident.

Goethe's heart leaped to his throat as he thought of what would have happened if the SS had discovered the transmitter. When he was sure no one was watching, he threw it into the River Seine.

Goethe had not seen Kani Ben-Ahr since he'd learned that she was the notorious Carmen, and he was glad. He was certain that the SS were not completely satisfied as to his innocence, and if he had seen her again, the SS would surely have arrested him.

Now, however, he needed desperately to see her. Goethe had found out that the SS knew where Carmen would be that evening. They had been informed by a collaborator that Kani Ben-Ahr would be at the Cafe du Dome at some time this evening. The SS would be waiting for her there.

At first, Ernst decided to let Kani go to her fate. After all, she had certainly been indifferent to the problems she'd caused him. If the SS had found that radio, they might have tortured him for information he truly couldn't have provided. They would have tortured him, and they would have killed him.

Ernst shivered as he thought of that. Then he thought of that same torturing being applied to Kani Ben-Ahr, and he shivered again. She was much too beautiful a créature to have to endure such barbarity. He would have to do something. He would have to warn her.

But how? If he showed up at the Cafe du Dome tonight, the SS would know why he was there. He had to get word to her somehow, but how does one go about contacting the spy of an enemy country, when that spy knows that she is known?

Marcel Garneau.

Ernst didn't know why he never realized this simple truth before now. Obviously Marcel Garneau was aware of Kani Ben-Ahr's espionage activities. Kani spent a great deal of time at the cafe, and she and Marcel and his daughter seemed to be great friends. In fact, Ernst thought, it wouldn't surprise him at all if Marcel was himself an underground fighter, if not a spy. If that were so, then Marcel might be able to get word to Kani.

Ernst hurried to Marcel's Cafe.

Marcel's was not nearly as crowded as it was before the invasion. In the early days of the German occupation, every table had been filled with German soldiers and French girls, and there were many fine discussions of art and few of politics. Now there were a few French civilians and no soldiers at all. For a moment Ernst felt a spasm of fear. If Marcel was an underground fighter, wouldn't this be an excellent opportunity to kill a German soldier?

Marcel smiled at Ernst, the same smile he had shown every time Ernst had come into the place. It was somewhat disconcerting. He either meant the smile now, when Ernst was part of an army in retreat, or he had not meant it earlier, when Ernst was one of the triumphant ones.

"Major Goethe, it is good to see you again after so long a time," Marcel said. "Where have you been?"

"I've been keeping busy," Ernst said. "The way of the army is incomprehensible . . . They have required the filming of the defeats, as surely as they wanted filming of the victories."

"Defeat? Is that any way for a German officer to talk?" Marcel asked. "The allies have moved quickly into the countryside, but it may just be a temporary setback for your army."

Ernst laughed, but it was a small laugh without mirth. "You and I both know we are not talking about a temporary setback, Marcel. We are defeated in France . . . We may even be defeated in this war. You should be happy; the invaders are leaving your country."

"Well," Marcel said carefully, "I've never made any secret of the fact that I would prefer the Germans to go home."

"You don't hate all the Germans, do you, Marcel? Some of us were caught up in this thing, and we were as much the victims as the French. I, for one, have long had a distaste for the war, and especially for the excesses of the brutish SS men."

"You have always behaved decently in my establishment," Marcel said.

Ernst smiled. "There are many other Germans just like me," he said. "You will see, after the war, when many of us can become friends again. I am an artist, Marcel, and this place is a haven for artists. I will come back in happier times."

"I will look forward to such a time," Marcel said.

Ernst looked around the cafe, studying the faces of everyone there.

"Are you looking for someone?" Marcel asked.

"These people," Ernst said. "Are they all known to you?"

Marcel looked around.

"Yes," he said. "I know them all."

"I wish to say something," Ernst said. "If the words are heard by the wrong person, it could be very dangerous."

"For whom would it be dangerous?" Marcel asked.

"For me," Ernst said. "And for you as well."

Marcel stood up. "I have very little of that sausage left," he said in a voice louder than the voice he had been using. "What I do have is in my kitchen. Come, I will show you."

Ernst stood up and walked back toward the kitchen with Marcel. Marcel opened a box and began cutting off a piece of sausage.

"I know them all," he said. "But I do not

know everyone's politics. Sometimes one can be quite surprised."

"Yes," Ernst said. "As I was by Kani Ben-Ahr."

Marcel handed Ernst a piece of the sausage, and Ernst put it in his mouth, then smacked his lips appreciatively. "I didn't know there was anything like this left in the city," he said seriously.

"What did you wish to tell me?" Marcel asked.

"Where is Kani Ben-Ahr?"

"I don't know," Marcel said. "Kani Ben-Ahr turned out to be an espionage agent. But of course, you know that, don't you?"

"I have had to answer to the SS for befriending her," Ernst said. "They are a most uncouth lot."

"I have heard stories," Marcel said. "But why do you want to find Kani Ben-Ahr? Do you want to turn her over to the SS?"

"No, of course not," Ernst said. "In fact, I would like to find her so I can prevent that. She is in great danger."

"Of course, she is in danger," Marcel said. "The SS has discovered that Kani Ben-Ahr is the one called Carmen."

"No," Ernst said. "Her danger is even greater than that."

"What do you mean?"

"Tonight," Ernst said, "Kani Ben-Ahr is expected to show up at the Cafe du Dome. The SS will be there waiting for her. Marcel, you *must* get word to her. She must not show up."

"My friend," Marcel said, "what makes you think I have any way of getting word to her?"

"I . . . I don't know that you can," Ernst said. "But you are most resourceful, and I can only hope that your resourcefulness will find some means to warn Kani. I would not want to see her subjected to SS torture."

"I may know a friend who knows a friend," Marcel said. "I'll see what I can do."

$\mathbf{P}$hillip Hornsby had tried four escapes since becoming a prisoner of war. All four had failed. Now he was appearing before Colonel Dawes and the escape committee with a fifth plan. He was determined that this plan would not fail.

The escape committee was in Colonel Dawes' room, but Colonel Dawes himself had not yet arrived. Phil was sitting on the floor, waiting for him, as the committee members talked among themselves.

"I'll tell you that I, for one, am quite opposed to granting this man another go," one of the men was saying to the others. "Every time there is an unsuccessful attempt, that avenue of escape is closed, so that another and perhaps more capable fellow is denied that chance. Lieutenant Hornsby has tried four times, and he has failed four times. I think it is time to let a few of the other lads have a chance and to keep Hornsby on the back burner for a while.''

"And I say that our only function is to review the plans, then offer advice," another said. "We don't have the right to pass judgment on the individuals, nor do we have the right to disapprove of anyone attempting to escape.''

The door opened, and Colonel Dawes stepped into the room. He walked quickly to the window, looked out, then turned to face the others. There were four people in the room from the escape committee, plus Phillip Hornsby.

Dawes smiled broadly.

"Lads, as you know, I've been in the office of the camp commandant to complain about our food. And. . . ." he let the sentence hang.

"Don't tell me Jerry is going to improve our food?''

"Better than that," Colonel Dawes said. He rubbed his hands together and smiled more broadly than before. "Lads, Paris has been taken by the Allies.''

"What? Colonel Dawes, are you sure?''

"Absolutely. The Germans have withdrawn from Paris and are in full retreat. There are one million

Allied soldiers on the continent and more on the way.''

"What do you think this means?" one of the men asked.

"Why, I can tell you what it means. It means the war will be over in a matter of weeks, that's what it means! Lads, our long nightmare is almost over!"

The others started to cheer, but Colonel Dawes quickly shushed them.

"I think it might be better," he said, "if we don't let Jerry know that we know. There is one possibility that we must face and be prepared for.''

"What is that?"

Colonel Dawes cleared his throat. "If the Germans realize that the Allies are nearly upon them, they may decide that the best thing to do with us would be to . . .''

"Kill us?" someone asked quietly.

Colonel Dawes nodded his head.

"My God, you don't really think they would do such a thing, do you?"

"We must face that possibility," Colonel Dawes said. "Now, they would have to try and surprise us, because I don't think they could bring it off smoothly otherwise. Therefore, we should be prepared, and have a plan of resistance. If the Jerries don't know that we know, then our chances of a successful resistance are greatly increased.''

"Right.''

"My suggestion is that we form a resistance committee to come up with a plan that might work. Now, what have we here? Another escape attempt, Phil?"

"I'm certain he won't want to go through with it now," one of the others said. "Not with the Germans in full retreat. I mean, there's no sense in risking an attempt, is there? If we just sit tight, our lads will be coming up to the front door."

"Unless the Germans do decide to do us all in," Phil said.

"Well, I don't really think they will, do you, Colonel?"

"No, I don't," Colonel Dawes said. "But I don't want any nasty surprises either, and that's why I want us to prepare."

"There, you see? No need to get all upset. Just sit tight and wait it out."

"No," Phil said sharply. "I'm going to try again, with or without your approval. You can't prevent me from trying."

"No, of course, we can't prevent you," Colonel Dawes said. "But remember, the purpose of the escape committee is to help you, to provide you with German money, identification papers, emergency rations, and that sort of thing. It's not likely we'll disapprove your plan as long as it doesn't endanger anyone else. I can't help but think, though, that with this new development you might be better off waiting."

266

"No, I want to try another escape," Phil said firmly.

"Very well," Colonel Dawes said. He looked at the others. "This meeting is officially opened. Lieutenant, let me hear your plan."

Phil smiled. "I've been working on it for over a month now," he said. He pulled a piece of paper from his shirt pocket, unfolded it, and showed it to Colonel Dawes and the others.

"What is this?" Colonel Dawes asked. "I don't understand."

"It's a false firewall," Phil explained. "All I have to do is raise the bonnet of the correct model scout motorcar, climb in behind the motor, then fit this artificial firewall into position over me. Then, even when the bonnet is lifted, I can't be seen, unless someone makes a terribly close examination of the firewall."

"But won't that false firewall be awfully close to the motor?" someone asked.

"Yes, though I've machined it to the closest tolerance possible."

"How close?"

"The firewall will be only fourteen inches from the actual firewall."

"Can you fit into a space that small?" Colonel Dawes asked.

"It will be a very close squeeze, but I can do it," Phil said.

"How will you find the time to get the firewall

attached?'' someone asked. "It will require several minutes just to fit all the screws, won't it?''

"No," Phil said. "I've designed quick fasteners, rather like the dzus fasteners used on the engine nacelles of aircraft. I can have the entire firewall in position in less than thirty seconds. I only have one problem, and it shouldn't be too serious."

"What problem is that?"

"I think I can answer that question," Colonel Dawes said. "You'll need someone to put the bonnet back down once you are safely inside, right?"

"That's correct, sir. Once I have the firewall in place, I can't reach the bonnet. I thought I might just leave it up, and when the driver returns, he could put it back down."

"But he might get suspicious as to why it is up and decide to make a close examination," Colonel Dawes said.

"Yes, sir."

"Then you are going to have to have someone help you."

"But that would involve someone else in the escape plot," one of the others protested. "And with nothing to gain personally, the risk of getting caught does not seem to justify the involvement."

"If someone would voluntarily take that risk, then you would have no say in the matter, would you?" Phil challenged.

"If someone would voluntarily assume the risk. But who would be so foolish?"

"Perhaps I have just such a person in mind," Colonel Dawes asked.

"You know someone, Colonel?" Phil asked, his mood growing brighter with the prospect of having his plan approved.

"Yes," the Colonel said. He looked at the plan for a long moment, then he looked at Phil and smiled. "I'll do it."

The others gasped.

"You?" one of them asked. "But Colonel Dawes, why would you do such a thing?"

"I'm not sure, really," Colonel Dawes said. "Perhaps it's because I have admiration for any man who is willing to go back and try a fifth time. Look at me, I've been here for four years, and I've never tried once."

"But that's different. You are the inspiration for all of us. The men of the camp look up to you, and need you."

Colonel Dawes shook his head. "No," he said. "No, that isn't really true. I've told myself that, and I've tried to delude myself—and others—with the idea that I was of more service to my country here than if I tried to escape. The truth is, though, that I haven't tried because, quite frankly, I have been too frightened."

"Colonel, that isn't true!"

Colonel Dawes held up his hand.

"Don't try to tell me what is true and what isn't. I've had four years of opportunity for reflection. There has been plenty of time for such thoughts here, and I've come to a rather unflattering conclusion about myself. I decided that it was much easier to sit the war out here than to take a chance on being shot while trying to escape . . . or . . . to go back flying bombing missions and letting every fighter pilot in Germany try to make me his next kill. Perhaps it's a little late in the game for a sudden declaration of courage and a little late for me to correct the mistakes I have made. But, for what it is worth, Lieutenant, I believe your plan has a good chance for success, and I would like to help you. Perhaps I can even share vicariously in your triumph when you pull it off."

"Thank you, Colonel," Phil said, still in shock that Colonel Dawes had agreed to help him. He had never considered his relationship with Colonel Dawes that good. Phil was always trying to escape, and would have attempted it every day if the opportunity had presented itself, while Colonel Dawes, on the other hand, had continuously urged caution and restraint. By their very natures they had been at cross-purposes. Now Phil's success would depend upon Colonel Dawes' help. It would mean that Colonel Dawes would have to defy his own code and take a maximum risk with no chance of personal gain. The odds were bad.

"Well, gentlemen, I propose that Lieutenant

Hornsby's plan be approved. Do I hear any objections? None?'' He said it so quickly that no one had a chance to object. ''Good, then the plan stands approved. Phil, when do you want to try?''

''Now,'' Phil said.

''Now?''

Phil smiled. ''I was going to go anyway. If the committee disapproved, I was going to leave before you realized it.'' He pointed through the window. ''There's the motorcar. The courier arrived about half an hour ago. He's waiting for the dispatches. They will be ready at ten hundred hours sharp. At 0955, the courier will drive the car to the latrine, go inside for four minutes, then go over to the headquarters building for the dispatches. While he is using the latrine, the motorcar is out of everyone's view. That is when I will get into position.''

''How do you know he will go to the latrine today?''

''He goes every day, just before he picks up the dispatches. He is a man of precise habits.''

Colonel Dawes smiled. ''I'll bet you never thought your freedom would depend upon the regularity of a German's bowels.''

''No, sir,'' Phil replied, returning the Colonel's grin. ''But I'll take opportunity wherever I can.''

''Where is the artificial firewall?'' Colonel Dawes asked. ''I would like to take a look at it.''

"It is in the prisoner latrine," Phil said. "I've shaped it around the bottom of one of the lavatories."

"Then let's do it, shall we?" Colonel Dawes said. "Gentlemen, give Lieutenant Hornsby the money, rations and work papers."

One of the men from the escape committee pulled a board away from Colonel Dawes' wall and removed a carefully wrapped package. When the package was unwrapped, it disclosed a total of nearly thirty pounds in various monies—German, French, English and American. There was a small packet of dried fruit and a handful of malt tablets. There were also some papers identifying him as a conscript worker from France. He was expected to furnish his own clothes, and Phil, like the others who planned escapes, already had the clothes he would need.

Phil slipped out of his uniform to disclose the clothes he wore beneath. They were typical of the conscript workers' clothes, a shirt and pants of coarse weave.

"Don't you think you should keep part of your uniform?" Colonel Dawes asked. "As long as you are wearing any part of it, you can't legally be classified as an espionage agent."

"Yes," one of the other members of the committee pitched in. "I would strongly recommend that you wear your uniform under your clothes."

"If you gentlemen will excuse me," Phil said, "you strongly recommended that the last time—

and the time before that, and the times before that. But, this time, I am not going to wear any of the uniform. Twice before I would have made it to freedom, had not some part of my uniform given me away. This time, I'm going all the way. I'll either make it to freedom, or I'll be killed, but I'll *not* spend another day in this place."

Phil put the money in his pocket and the emergency rations under his shirt. Then he shook hands with each of the escape committee members. While they were shaking hands, the sound of the car engine reached them.

"Gentlemen, time and Sergeant Jahnke's bowels wait for no man," Phil quipped. "Colonel Dawes, sir, if you are going to assist me in this operation, I strongly suggest that you do it now."

"Right you are, old man," Colonel Dawes said with a smile.

Colonel Dawes and Phil slipped through the back door, then strolled casually toward the latrine area. They appeared to be engaged in a spirited campaign, and, for the sake of anyone who overheard them, they were talking about the relative merits of various English football teams.

When they reached the latrine area, almost as an afterthought, Phil asked the Colonel to wait for him while he went inside. Colonel Dawes tried to look as if he was merely waiting for a friend, although, in fact, he was alert to the slightest movement that might indicate trouble.

Inside the latrine, Phil went directly to one of the lavatories and knelt beneath the sink, then turned a few hand-fastened fittings. A formed piece of tin dropped down, and he took it outside.

"Where did you get the metal?" Colonel Dawes asked, when he saw Phil's handiwork.

"I filched a couple of jerry cans from the Jerries," Phil answered with a laugh.

"I must confess that it is a beautiful job," Colonel Dawes said. "I congratulate you on your workmanship."

"Would you believe that as a boy I was totally incapable of using my hands in any sort of craft?" Phil said. "I couldn't even make a model airplane." He looked at his artificial firewall. "I don't mind telling you that I am more than a little proud of it. I almost wish someone would have to examine it; I should like to test it."

"Don't flirt with disaster over a misguided case of pride in workmanship," Colonel Dawes said. "That's foolish vanity."

"You are right," Phil said. He laughed. "I wasn't really serious anyway. Come on, let's get this thing installed."

Phil and Colonel Dawes stepped up to the small scout car and raised the hood. Phil climbed up behind the engine, then, with the Colonel's help, fitted the firewall over himself. The holes for the lines and rods were perfectly aligned, and it looked as natural as the real wall.

"How does it look?" Phil asked, his voice muffled by his invention.

"It looks wonderful," Dawes said. "Quiet, here comes Jahnke. It's too late to put the hood down, he's seen me."

"Colonel," Jahnke called, as he approached the car buttoning his pants. He hurried from a leisurely stroll to a quick gait as he hastened over to the car.

"Good morning, Sergeant Jahnke," Colonel Dawes said calmly.

"Here, what are you doing under the hood of my car?" Sergeant Jahnke asked excitedly. "You cannot touch my car. It is strictly forbidden. You know this."

"Relax, Sergeant," Colonel Dawes said easily. "I was just admiring the German workmanship. I have to hand it to you blighters, you are mechanical whizzes. This is a marvelous engine."

"Ja, ist gut," Jahnke said. "Are you certain you do nothing to the car? You make no mischief?"

Colonel Dawes laughed. "I did nothing to the engine," he said. He held his hands up. "Here, look for yourself if you wish."

Jahnke slammed the hood closed. "I have no time now," he said. "I must go now for the dispatches. However, Colonel, if I have trouble with my engine, I will remember that I saw you here, and it shall go very badly for you."

"You shall have no trouble, Sergeant, I assure

275

you," Colonel Dawes said. "At least, no trouble which I caused."

Jahnke got into the car and started it, almost hesitantly, as if he were afraid that something might explode. He raced the engine a few times, and then, convinced that nothing was wrong, he drove over to the headquarters building and dashed inside for the dispatches.

Beneath the hood of the car, Phil lay in a cramped position and scarcely dared to breathe. He waited patiently until Sergeant Jahnke came back out of the building, got in the car and drove away.

Phil had planned for everything except the heat. The purpose of the real firewall was to prevent the heat of the engine from passing through to the passenger compartment, but Phil's artificial firewall did little toward insulating him from the heat. In fact, it seemed to conduct the heat with exceptional efficiency, and the temperature in the close quarters behind the fake firewall climbed dramatically. Phil began to fear that he might die of heat prostration if he had to ride too far.

The ride seemed interminable, and the heat built up more and more. The conditions were becoming unbearable, and Phil was finding it more and more difficult to breathe.

Suddenly, he felt the driver slam on the brakes. The car went into a skid; then there was a low thud of an explosion and the car rolled over and over. The hood popped open, and Phil felt himself being dumped out. Miraculously, the car flipped in such a way as to avoid crushing him, and he was left lying on the ground as the car continued to roll down an embankment and finally exploded in flames.

Phil heard the roar of aircraft engines then, and he looked up to see two fighter aircraft diving for him. He saw the red, white and blue concentric circles which were the wing insignia of the R.A.F. He waved happily, but the planes fired at him.

"I'm British, you bloody idiots!" Phil shouted, waving his fist at his attackers, giving vent to his frustration and rage. He yelled, even though he knew they couldn't hear him.

Fortunately both planes missed. Then, because they considered one man on foot an unworthy target for the expenditure of fuel and ammunition required for another pass, they flew on.

With the immediate danger gone, Phil looked around to get his bearings. He knew he should move west. He had no idea how far the invasion had advanced, but common sense told him that if he went west far enough, he would eventually hook up with his own people.

In England, the citizens of London were now coping with Hitler's latest and most terrifying weapon: the V-2 bomb. Like the V-1, the V-2 was pilotless, and so could exact the maximum damage with the minimum risk of life to the attacker. But the V-2 had several new and more frightening aspects.

The V-1 was actually a pilotless aircraft. It was propelled by a pulse-jet engine, and it was very fast, though a Spitfire, with a good angle, could overtake it and shoot it down, or else tip its wings so that the V-1's gyro tumbled. When that happened, the guidance system was fouled, and the V-1 would veer away from London and often crash into the sea.

The V-2 was not a pilotless aircraft; it was a rocket. It approached London from outside the earth's atmosphere at speeds in excess of three thousand miles per hour. It made no tell-tale buzzing sound, and the English radar system could not detect its approach. The Londoners called it 'silent death,' for those who were killed by it never even knew it was coming.

The V-2s were guided to London by a targeting system which was quite sophisticated, but, once over London, there was no way to determine where they would fall. Factories, homes, hospitals, schools, even open fields, were likely to be struck.

So were hotels, and one such hotel, converted to special apartments for American officers, was hit at 0300 hours in the morning. The rocket killed fourteen American officers and one British civilian.

The Britisher's presence at the hotel puzzled the authorities at first, because it was a woman and there should not have been any women on the premises at that hour of the morning. It was finally concluded that the woman must have been engaged in an illicit affair with one of the officers; it was an indiscretion that cost her her life.

It was some time before the young woman's identity was ascertained, and when the authorities did learn her name, it was decided to inform her family, but not to make a public announcement. After all, the bereaved family had suffered enough without adding the embarrassment of their daughter's conduct to their misery.

16

"**H**old it right there, Mac! Just where the hell do you think you're goin' anyway?"

The speaker was a young American soldier, and he had spotted Phil creeping slowly through a ditch alongside a road.

When Phil heard the English words, albeit with an American accent, he heaved a sigh of relief and stood up.

"Thank God, I've made it," he said. "I'm Lieutenant Phillip Hornsby, would you please take me to . . ."

"Get your hands up, buddy, or I'll shoot you where you stand," the soldier ordered.

"What?" Phil questioned, unable to believe that the soldier was still suspicious. "Look here, old man, we're supposed to be allies. You are American, aren't you?"

"I'm American all right," the soldier said. "That ain't the question. The question is, what the hell are you?"

"My God, don't you hear me speaking English?"

"Yeah," the soldier said. "And it don't sound like no English I ever heard."

"Look," Phil said in exasperation. "Is there an intelligence officer you could take me to? Or even someone who is intelligent?"

"Sarge!" the American soldier called. "Sarge, come here, I got me someone!"

"How 'bout that?" another voice said, as a second man appeared from the woodline on the opposite side of the road. Phil noticed then that a squad of American soldiers seemed to be camped in the woodline.

"Sergeant, would you inform this bloody idiot that I am *not* a German?" Phil asked.

"Lissen to 'im talk, Sarge," the soldier said. "Don't he talk funny?"

"Young man, you should be listening to your slaughter of my native language through *my* ears," Phil said.

The sergeant laughed. "He's English," he said. "Ain't you never heard no Limey talk?"

The soldier lowered his rifle slightly. "Ain't

never heard nobody talk like that in Missouri,'' he said. ''Wait a minute, didn't the Cap'n say the Germans was sneakin' some English talkin' sappers through our lines?''

-''I assure you, I am *not* a German sapper,'' Phil said. ''I am Lieutenant Phillip Hornsby of the Royal Air Force. I have just escaped from a German prisoner of war camp, and I would like to be returned to the British lines.''

''All right, buddy, if you're really on our side, tell me about the St. Louis Cardinals,'' the young soldier who had captured him demanded.

''The St. Louis Cardinals? I'm sorry, I'm Anglican, and I don't know anything about the Roman Church groups.''

''Sarge, this guy's a phony, see? I could tell that right off. We got us a German sapper!''

The sergeant laughed. ''Because he doesn't know about the St. Louis Cardinals? Hell, Karnes, the English don't know nothin' about baseball.'' He turned to Phil. ''Okay, Limey, I'll tell you what I'll do. I'll take you on back to our Division C.P. They'll know what to do with you.''

''Thank you,'' Phil said, relieved that the lunacy seemed to be over.

Phil walked about half a mile with the two men the sergeant had assigned to take him back. He had been allowed to lower his hands, and one of them had given him a cigarette, but both still kept loaded rifles ready. They finally reached a small field where several tents and vehicles were gathered into what the American's called a C.P., or Command Post. There Phil was turned over to an American Major.

"Are you hungry?" the major asked, as the two soldiers returned to their positions.

"Rather," Phil said. "I've had only a raw potato in the last two days."

The major tossed Phil a small, olive-green tin. "Beans and franks," he said. "They're about the best C ration we have."

"Lovely," Phil said, examining the tin. "How does one get the bloody thing open?"

The major laughed, then removed his identity tags. A small can-opener was hanging from the chain, and he took the beans and franks back from Phil, quickly opened them, and handed them back to him. "Here," he said. "You'll need a spoon."

Phil began eating, and the taste of real food after several days of scrounging was wonderful. He ate ravenously.

"Say, there's a Limey—uh, *British* General in camp right now. He's coordinating logistics with our C.G. I'll make arrangements to send you back to the British lines with him, if you'd like."

"Of course," Phil said. He put the empty can down. "Thank you, Major, that was quite delicious."

"You'll still have to return under guard," the major said. "Until we have proof of your identity,

284

we have to be careful. The Germans have infiltrated our lines with English-speaking sappers. The men are very shaky about it."

"I know," Phil said. "I discovered that when I encountered one of your chaps who had never heard my accent in Missouri."

The major laughed, then looked up as a couple of officers approached.

"I hear you have a man here who claims to be an English flier," one of the men said. His accent was definitely British, but that wasn't what made Phil look around so quickly. It was something else . . . a recognized tremor to the speaker's voice.

The speaker saw Phil, then he smiled broadly. "Phil! Thank God, you are safe!"

"You know this man, General?" the major asked in surprise.

"Know him?" General Whiteacre replied. "Young man, he is my son-in-law!"

"How is Karen?" Phil asked.

"Anxious to introduce you to your son," General Whiteacre answered with a broad smile.

"My son?"

"Phillip Cairns Hornsby. He looks just like you, Phil."

Phil smiled. "He'd better."

17

It was January 5th, 1945. High in the crystal blue sky over Western Europe, a formation of sixtyfour B-17G bombers beat their way through the rarefied stratosphere toward their target deep inside war-torn Germany. Most of the bombers sported flamboyant names, and many had tiny bombs painted on the fuselage to indicate the number of previous missions flown. The name of one of the planes was *Truculent Turtle II,* and beneath the name, which was done in script, was a cartoonist's rendition of a large turtle wearing an officer's service cap, which was crushed at the sides by an oversized headset. The turtle stared ahead with a ferocious scowl, and guns bristled from beneath his chin and from his shell in approximately the same places guns were bristling from the bomber itself.

Just behind the turtle were three painted rows of ten bombs each, and one row of eight, denoting a mission history which began with the great 'Black Thursday' Schweinfurt raid sixteen months earlier and ended with an attack on Berlin the previous week. Behind the rows of bombs more information was stenciled in a cold, impersonal way:

A/C SERIAL NUMBER: 324459
FOR RESCUE CUT HERE
Fire Extinguishers Located at
Stations: 115, 430 and 610
Service this aircraft with
115/145
Crew Chief: T/Sgt. Donald L.
Weeks
Pilot: Captain Martin W.
Holt

Martin had also been the pilot of the original *Truculent Turtle*, in which he flew sixteen missions before being shot down over France on the way back from a raid. Those missions weren't reflected in the bomb count on the side of this aircraft, so Martin's actual personal total stood at fifty-four, making him one of the most experienced pilots in the entire wing.

Inside the *Truculent Turtle II*, Martin pulled and tugged at his oxygen mask in a futile attempt to relieve the discomfort of the sweat. Though the outside air temperature was minus-forty degrees, the close-fitting mask had caused his face to sweat, and the sweat had gathered and pooled at the chin cup of the mask, irritating him and causing unbearable itching. Martin wanted to jerk the mask off and wipe his chin, but he couldn't. He didn't dare remove the mask because they were flying at 25,000 feet, and at this altitude his lungs could burst if they were denied the equalizing pressure of the forced oxygen.

"I mustn't think about it," Martin said aloud. He often spoke aloud during the long flights, but, as he didn't key the mike button, none of the other members of his crew could hear him. Therefore, he was able to engage in this habit without being discovered. "If I can just get my mind off the problem, the problem will go away," he said. "I must think of something else. It's worked before; it will work again."

Martin scanned the sky around him, looked out at the planes which were flying in the standard 'combat box' formation. As missions went, this was a relatively small one. Martin had been in raids which consisted of more than three hundred airplanes. But that was in '43 and '44, when there were still many targets worthy of such operations. This was 1945, and there were very few German cities which had not been reduced to rubble by nearly three years of bombing around the clock—Americans by day and British by night. As the targets became fewer and fewer, so did the mission requirements.

The target for today's mission was Nuremberg.

"It is a psychological target," General Busby, their Group Commanding General, had told them at three o'clock this morning when they gathered in the briefing room, still clinging to paper cups of coffee and trying to fight off the damp, penetrating English cold.

"Did you say it was a psychological target, General?" one of the pilots asked.

"Yes, I did."

"Excuse my ignorance, sir, but what the hell is a psychological target?"

Several of the others laughed nervously at the pilot's question, but they listened closely to the answer, because he had asked the question many of them wanted answered.

"It is simply this," General Busby replied. "The Nuremberg marshalling yards have all been destroyed, the factories neutralized, and there are no military installations there. But the city is one of the most important cities in the entire Nazi psychological make-up, home of the rallies and all that. We feel we can undermine their will to fight by reducing the city to rubble. That would hasten the end of the war.''

Martin thought about General Busby's words. He had bombed the submarine pens at Wilhemshaven, the aircraft factories at Wurzburg, the ball bearing plants at Schweinfurt and the rocket bases at Peenemunde. The flak and fighter resistance over those targets had been terrible, and on many of those missions the Americans had lost more than one-third of their attacking force. But Martin could see a reason for those attacks, and he felt justified in dropping the bombs. To Martin's mind, the psychological attack on Nuremberg was little more than the wholesale slaughter of civilians, and he did not like to think about that.

Martin looked over at his new co-pilot. His former co-pilot had been given his own airplane, and Martin had drawn a second lieutenant from Iowa who was flying his very first mission. His name was Walter Kindig, and his biggest fear had been that the war would end before he was able to drop any bombs on Germany. Kindig had been in a state of elation since early this morning when they took off from Wimbleshoe.

Wimbleshoe, Martin thought. That was such a typical English name, like Straffordshire and Ingersall Hall. Like Allison Cairns-Whiteacre. Where was Allison right now, this very moment? Was she thinking of him at this moment the way he was thinking of her? Could love really bridge time and distance better than a radio, so that people who were in love were really never apart, no matter how far their distance from one another?

Then there was Yolinda. They were never really together, no matter how close they were physically. What was she doing this very minute? In Illinois it was still before dawn, so she was probably in bed. Was she alone?

"Cap'n, I have a fix," Manny said, cutting through the static of Martin's earphones. Manny was Manny Byrd, the only other member of Martin's crew who was still with him from the original *Truculent Turtle*. He, like Martin, was a captain, and he was the navigator.

"Go ahead, Manny," Martin said.

"We are 180 miles out on a 285 radial from the target. Our ground speed is 205 miles-per-hour, and ETA to the aiming point is fifty-two minutes."

"Roger. Pilot to crew, we are fifty-two minutes from target. Be on the alert."

Before they reached their destination, they received a target change from the weather recon flight, which informed them that the cloud cover over Nuremberg was 7/10ths. The secondary target was to be Schweinfurt, scene of repeated raids against the ball-bearing plants, but still a legitimate choice as an alternate. The truth was, however, that if there had been no alternate, the bombers would have unloaded their bombs anywhere, even over a small village or a farmer's field, just to get rid of them. That was absolutely necessary, for without eliminating the weight of the bombs, the bomber would not have enough fuel to get back to Wimbleshoe.

Unfortunately for the men in the attacking bombers, the German Air Defense Command had correctly guessed the target to be Schweinfurt, with Nuremberg under heavy cloud cover. They were, therefore, able to concentrate all their remaining fighter aircraft and flak batteries in such a way as to maximize their effectiveness.

The highway in the sky which stretched from Nuremberg to Schweinfurt became a pathway through the valley of death. Anti-aircraft artillery was manned by experienced gunners, men who wanted desperately to extract their pound of flesh from the flying devils who had turned their country into a living hell. They launched welcoming cards into the formation in the form of exploding shells— angry, blinding flashes of light, flame, steel splinters and red-hot chunks of jagged metal.

Martin was a little surprised at the violence of the sky. It had been several missions since the Germans had been able to mount a defense this tenacious. Shell fragments were everywhere, slamming into engine nacelles to interrupt the delicate balance of moving parts which had been machined to tolerances of thousandths of an inch, or puncturing fuel tanks to ignite gasoline, or tearing holes through the plexiglass and aluminum skin to attack the men themselves, to sever arms, and legs, and to open torsos that spilt blood and intestines on the alclad.

One of the planes near the *Truculent Turtle II* took a direct hit in the bombbay, and the thirteen five-hundred-pound bombs went up instantly. There was a flash of light and a gigantic shock wave, but little wreckage, because the heat and shock very nearly vaporized the thirty-ton machine and the ten human beings within.

Mercifully, the flak disappeared as abruptly as it had begun, and once again the sky was blue and clear and welcoming.

After the flak came the fighters. All the machine guns on the *Truculent Turtle II* which could come to bear on the attacking fighters opened up, and the roar drowned out even the sound of the screaming engines. The first wave flashed by, rolling over to plunge through the combat box and avoid the deadly cross fire of the bombers they were attacking. The scream of the engines and the sounds of the guns, combined with the deep rumble of the bomber engines and the cries of the men, blended into a bizarre and cacaphonous symphony which could have been orchestrated in hell.

Suddenly there was the sound of metal on metal, and then the windshield cracked. A shell fragment smashed through and landed on Martin's lap.

"Oh my god! We're hit, we're hit!" Kindig shouted.

Martin looked down and saw the spent casing of a fifty caliber round. "Take it easy," he shouted. "We aren't hit! It's a spent casing from one of our own bombers flying in formation above us."

Kindig, who had covered his eyes with his arm, looked at the shell casing and laughed. It was a wild, hysterical laugh, but one which Martin easily recognized. He had laughed in the same way many times.

Then came the chunking sound of an actual hit, and the right outboard engine started going wild. Martin heard the banshee wail first, then felt the vibration as the engine threatened to pull out of the wing. He looked down at the tachometer and saw the RPM going through 3500 and still climbing. The prop governor was shot out and they had a runaway prop. To make matters worse, there was no way the propeller could be feathered.

"We're going to lose that prop," Martin said matter-of-factly.

"It'll come right through the side of the ship!" Kindig said, his voice rising in anxious excitement. "It's going to cut us to pieces!"

"No, it won't," Martin said. "Keep your eyes on it. The moment you see it start to go, let me know."

"What are you going to do?" Kindig asked. "You can't stop it."

"No time to explain now," Martin said. "Just let me know!"

The runaway prop was on number four, on Kindig's side of the plane. He sat in his seat with his eyes glued to the prop, oblivious of the screaming fighters and exploding shells around them. Finally he saw the telltale wobbling of the prop-shaft.

"It's going now!" he shouted. "It's cutting loose!"

Martin dropped the right wing just a little, then twisted hard to the left of the wheel and caused the right wing to flip up. It was timed perfectly, with the wing snapping up at the exact moment the propeller tore loose from the engine. The propeller's own momentum, plus the sudden upswing of the wing, tossed it harmlessly over the top of the airplane.

"You *did* it!" Kindig shouted joyously. "You *did* it!"

Even as Kindig was shouting in relief over losing the prop without sustaining any further damage, number three started spewing thick, oily black smoke. Fire leaped out from the nacelle and began caressing the wing root, licking at the skin which was less than one inch away from a thousand gallons of high octane gasoline.

"Damn!" Martin swore. "Hit the fire-bottle! Feather number three!"

Kindig pulled the fire extinguisher and hit the feather button. The smoke turned white, even as the propeller twisted into the wind and spun to a stop. When the smoke finally cleared away, the wrecked nacelle, white with scorching and residue from the extinguisher, told the graphic story of their predicament: two engines out, and the airplane was losing altitude.

"We're sitting ducks now," Martin said grimly. "I can't hold altitude and speed. We won't be able to stay in the box."

"Look!" Kindig shouted. "The Germans! They're heading away!"

"Well, it appears we might make it after all," Martin said.

"Is that Schweinfurt?" Kindig asked, pointing to a city before them.

Martin looked down at the familiar triangular shape of the small city nestled along the Main River. Around the outer edges of the town, long, graceful roads passed through peaceful-looking fields and by red-roofed houses in the small surrounding villages. As they drew closer to the city itself, they saw that there were fewer red roofs. A closer inspection showed that there were few roofs of any kind, because Schweinfurt had been such a frequent bombing target.

"Yeah," Martin said. "That's Pigtown."

"Pigtown? Why do you call it Pigtown?"

"Schweinfurt means swine ford, or 'pig crossing,' " Martin explained. "And it hasn't exactly been friendly to us over the last couple of years." Martin happened to glance up then, and he saw a bomber directly over them. "What the hell? What's he doing up there? Who is that, Walt, can you see his tail number?''

Kindig leaned forward in his seat and twisted around. ''It's Four-Six-Three,'' he said.

Martin switched the radio to plane to plane.

''Four-Six-Three, you are out of position. Get into your proper position.''

''This is Four-Six-Three. Who is calling me?''

''This is Four-Five-Nine, I'm just below you with two engines out. I've moved to the tuck position, but you're in my way.''

''I don't see you.''

''Well, hell, tell your ball gunner to stick his arm out and he can shake hands with my turret gunner. Now, get it on over.''

''Sorry,'' the other pilot said.

''Attention all planes, this is the flight leader. Salvo all bombs now.''

''No!'' Martin screamed, but he was too late, and thirteen bombs tumbled down from the airplane just above him. One of the bombs sliced through the tail of the *Truculent Turtle II* and cut the airplane in half. With full power on the two engines on the left wing, no power on the engines on the right wing and no control surfaces to overcome the pressures, the airplane went into an immediate flat spin. Martin's head was slammed against the steel frame of the armor-plated seat and everything went black.

*   *   *

George Thomas was standing beside Allison as the bombers touched down one by one. Allison was squeezing his hand very tightly.

"Oh, Jesus," one of the soldiers with the football said. "Oh, Jesus, the *Turtle* isn't with them. The *Turtle* didn't come back."

"The *Turtle?*" Allison said, overhearing the soldier's comment. She looked at George. "George, isn't Martin's aircraft called the *Truculent Turtle?*"

"That's my ship, ma'am," the soldier said. "I'm Sergeant Weeks, the ground crew chief."

"Sergeant Weeks, how can you be so certain that the *Truculent Turtle* isn't among the the returning aircraft?" George asked.

"Sir, you think a man can't tell his own ship? I'd be an awful poor crew chief if I couldn't pick her out of a formation. I'm tellin' you, she's not there."

"Oh, George, no!" Allison gasped. She felt her heart go up to her throat.

"Relax, Allison. He could be wrong."

Finally the last bomber sat down, and all began taxiing into position, the squeal of their brakes audible against the background thunder of the engines. Like ducks they came, one following another, moving so awkwardly on the ground, where but moments before they had been sleek, graceful birds in the air. The planes moved into their revetments; then the engines were killed, and the ready trucks began driving out to the planes.

"That's the *Turtle* revetment there," Sergeant Weeks said, pointing to a bay which was conspicuous by the absence of the airplane which should have been there. Over to one side lay a bicycle, left there that morning by one of the crew members who had pedaled out to the plane.

The ready trucks began coming back from the planes then, carrying the crewmen to the debriefing shacks. Suddenly, one of the trucks stopped, and a man jumped down and started toward Allison. His flying suit was unzipped, and his helmet hung loose with the electric and oxygen cords dangling like the tentacles of an octopus.

"Allison?" the man called.

Allison looked up at the sound of an American voice calling her name. She had a split second of irrational hope, and yet she knew it was irrational, and thus did not let it get the better of her.

The man who had called her was Brad Phillips. Allison knew Brad through Martin, and knew that he, like Martin, had been a football player in college. They had played against each other then, though recently they had become best of friends.

"Brad, oh Brad, Martin . . . is he . . ." Allison couldn't complete the sentence.

Brad shook his head sadly. "I'm sorry," he said.

"No! Oh Brad, no!" Allison wailed, the tears she had managed to control thus far now leaping to her eyes.

300

"What happened?" George asked. "Was it flak or fighters?"

"Neither," Brad said, shaking his head sadly. "That's the hell of it. One of the planes above Martin was out of position, and the bombs he dropped cut right through Martin's plane. Neither Martin nor his crew ever had a chance. There were no chutes."

George reached out for Allison, letting her come to him to cry her grief and sorrow. Her tears were bitter, the more so because now Martin would never know the wonderful secret she had been waiting to tell him. He would never know about the baby she would have for him.

18

THE NEW GERMANY IN A PEACE-
FUL EUROPE, read the headlines in one of
the newspapers in London's Heathrow Airport.
Other newspapers proclaimed peace in Europe
and spoke of the final days of Japan. Greg Waverly
glanced at them as he walked by the newspaper
stand.

"Pardon me, sir, but are you Major Gregory
Waverly?" a police officer asked.

Greg, leaning on the cane which would be a
permanent fixture in his life from now on, stopped
and looked up. He rubbed the back of his finger
across his closely-cropped moustache.

303

"Yes," he said. "I am Major Waverly. What can I do for you?"

The promotion of Major had come along with the Victoria Cross, the reward of a country "grateful for the many hardships and valorous deeds" Greg and his fellow 'Chindits' had undergone and performed.

Greg was one of the few survivors of his unit's foray deep into the Burmese jungles. He and his men had stayed there for two years. During that time his commander, General Wingate, had been killed, and forty-six of the sixty men who went into the jungles with him had died, either in enemy action or from the hazards of the jungle itself.

Greg had lost sixty-five pounds during his ordeal, and when he finally came out of the jungle, limping on a makeshift cane, he was nearly unrecognizable. A one-month stay in an Indian hospital and a diet which put weight back on his skeleton-like frame soon had him the robust man he was before. Only the knee, permanently damaged, reminded him of his long nightmare.

Greg had been met at the airport by a London police officer, and now, as he studied the man who had addressed him, he wondered why he had been singled out.

"I think you'd better come with me, sir," the policeman said.

"Come with you? Whatever for?"

"It's just routine, sir. Purely routine."

"Listen, if I learned one thing in this bloody war," Greg said, "it is that nothing is purely routine. Now you tell me why you want me to come with you, or you just get the hell out of my sight."

"It's about your wife, sir," the police officer said.

"My wife is dead," Greg said. "She was killed in a V-2 attack. What can you tell me about her?"

"Well, nothing, sir, except to confirm the fact that she is dead. But her personal effects have never been collected."

"What? Why not? Couldn't any of her family have collected them? Why have you let them remain this long?"

"Please, sir, if you would come with me, there are a few things we feel you must know. We are only trying to save you some embarrassment, you understand."

"Embarrassment?" Greg said. "What kind of embarrassment?"

"Major, do you really want to discuss all the details here?" the police officer asked. "I really think you would be more comfortable discussing them down at the station, in privacy."

"Where was my wife when she was killed?" Greg asked.

"She was in the Kimberly Hotel," the policeman said.

"And what time was she killed?"

"At about three in the morning."

"Three in the morning?"

"Yes, sir. You may be interested, sir, to know that the Kimberly Hotel was then being used as an American officers' quarters."

"I see," Greg said. He pinched the bridge of his nose for a long moment. "Very well, officer. I shall come with you."

"Greg! Greg, over here!" a woman's voice called, and Greg looked around to see Allison waving at him.

"Just a minute, officer," Greg said. He started toward Allison, and she ran to him. They met and embraced, then held each other silently for a long time. Finally, they parted, and when Greg looked again at Allison, he noticed her condition for the first time. "When is it due?" he asked.

"September," Allison said. She laughed a small, embarrassed laugh. "I'm the scandal of the family, you know. This baby shall have to add another hyphen to the family name."

"I gather you are not quite the family scandal," Greg said, turning away from Allison. "This rather insistent police officer has asked that I go to the police station with him. It seems that he has some secrets to bare about the situation surrounding Midge's death. Apparently she was in an American BOQ?"

"I am so sorry," Allison said. "It's bad enough to come home to her . . . dead . . . but to discover this about her . . . in such a way."

"Poor Midge," Greg said with a sigh. "I've never known an unhappier girl." He turned back to his sister-in-law. "How did you know I would be here, Allison?"

"I just kept calling until I found out," Allison said. "And then I was afraid I wouldn't get here in time to catch you. I didn't get here until well after your plane had landed. I have a car, by the way."

"Well, there is still the problem of this gentleman," Greg said, pointing to the policeman.

"Officer, is there any reason he can't ride with me?" Allison asked.

"No, miss, no reason at all," the officer said. "I was merely trying to provide a courtesy, that's all."

"I appreciate that," Greg said. "But if you don't mind, I'll ride with Lady Allison. I prefer to hear the details from my own people."

At the mention of Allison's title, the policeman straightened up and, almost subconsciously, came to attention. "Very good, sir," he said, saluting Greg.

Greg returned the salute, and when the policeman left, he went with Allison toward the car.

"Have you no luggage?" Allison asked.

Greg laughed and held up his cane. "Just this," he said. "And the shrapnel in my leg."

Greg followed Allison across the parking lot. He got into the car, slipping into the front seat next to her.

Allison started the car, put it into gear, then skillfully maneuvered through the congestion until she reached the main carriageway.

"I say, you do handle this machine nicely," Greg said with genuine appreciation for her skill.

"Thank you," Allison said. "I've had quite a little practice, you know. I've been driving Allied officers around for more than three years."

"Americans?"

"Yes," Allison said.

"The bastards."

"I'm sorry," Allison said. "I suppose you are quite put out with the Americans."

Greg laughed a short, bitter laugh. "No," he said. "It isn't their fault. I can't go through life hating every American I see, just because my wife was so stupid as to be killed in bed with one of them."

Greg was silent for a long moment, then sighed. "You know, Allison, I never should have left the jungle. It would be better off all around if I were still there keeping company with my friends."

"How can you say such a thing?" Allison asked.

308

"I left a number of good men there," Greg went on. "They're lying under the jungle sod. Their wars, public and private, are over. Mine goes on."

"After the cruelties of this war, I imagine many of the living are envying the dead," Allison said.

"Listen to me, feeling sorry for myself," Greg said, "as if I were the only one who's suffered." Greg looked at Allison. "If it's not too indelicate a question . . . where is the father?"

"Dead," Allison said.

"I'm sorry."

"He was an American."

"Now I'm really sorry," Greg said. "I had no right to spout off a moment ago. I hope you will forgive me."

"There's nothing to forgive," Allison said. "You have every right to be upset."

Allison reached over to squeeze Greg's hand. "There are some good things to talk about, though," she said. "Phil is back home, all safe and sound and enjoying the life of a father with his new little boy. Oh, and I don't suppose you heard about Mother."

"Lady Anne? What about her?"

Allison laughed. "Well, it seems that my dear mother, the very proper, very dignified, very staid Lady Anne, was up to her proper, dignified, staid elbows in espionage work."

"What?" Greg asked. He laughed. "For which side?"

Allison laughed with him and appreciated the fact that the atmosphere was now much less depressing.

"For our side, of course."

"What did she do?" Greg asked. "I mean, this is so incredible!"

"She trained radio operators and monitored their performance while they were in France, behind the enemy lines."

"Are you serious?"

"I'm quite serious," Allison said. "I met one of her 'girls,' who just returned, a lovely creature named Linda Starberg. You'll have to meet her sometime. She has the most marvelous stories to tell. But, of course . . . I'm sure you could tell a few hair-raising stories of your own."

"No," Greg said, "I have no stories to tell."

They were silent for the remainder of the drive, both of them lost in their own thoughts.

Greg looked out the window at the passing countryside. He recalled another time, a happier time, when he was young and dashing, a handsome lieutenant in the army of a glorious empire with all the world his oyster. Beside him, in that memory, was the loveliest pearl of that oyster—his new bride, Midge.

Allison Cairns-Whiteacre sat in the Lloyd George

chair in her bedroom and watched the sunset. The disc was blood-red and no longer painful to the eyes, and it spread its red and gold colors over the grounds of Ingersall Hall to backlight the beautifully sculptured hedgerows, statues and fountains. Its beauty was all the more poignant now, because Allison was looking at it alone. She would have given all she possessed to be able to reach over and take Martin's hand. But Martin wasn't here.

Allison had learned that Martin's body had been recovered and was being shipped to the United States. Yolinda would receive him in a flag-draped coffin.

Despite Allison's own sorrow, she couldn't help but feel sympathy for Yolinda. All Yolinda would have to show Dennis of his father would be that flag-draped coffin. Perhaps her own child would be better off for never having that as a memory.

There was a discreet knock at the door, and Allison heard Smythe call to her quietly. Smythe was evidence, if evidence were needed, that the war was finally over. He was the third generation of Smythes to enter 'the service' at Ingersall Hall, but he had been absent for the last five years fighting in the war. He had only been back a short time, and his return had been celebrated as much as the return of any of the members of the family.

"Yes, Smythe, come in," Allison called.

Smythe opened the door and stepped into the room.

"I beg your pardon, Lady Allison, but there is an American Officer here to see you."

"An American Officer? Who is it? Did he give you his name?"

"No, Lady Allison. He simply said he was a friend."

Allison got up from her Lloyd George chair, so called because Lloyd George was reputed to have once used this room and the chair was the only piece of original furniture remaining; and reached for the back of the chair to support herself. Her pregnancy was quite advanced now, and if she moved too abruptly, it caused a pain in her back. There were those who were still scandalized that Allison was to have a baby out of wedlock, but they didn't understand the significance of the baby. To Allison it was the one link she had with Martin, a part of him she could keep and love forever. Give up the baby? She would die first.

"I am Allison Cairns-Whiteacre," Allison said, as she stepped into the parlor a few moments later. A tall, handsome American lieutenant had been standing by the fireplace, and he turned as she entered. When he noticed her advanced pregnancy he hurried to offer her a chair.

"No, it's good for me to stand for a while," Allison said. She smiled in confusion. "Lieutenant, you'll have to forgive me. Have we ever met?"

"No," the lieutenant said. "Is the baby Martin's?"

"Who . . . who *are* you?" she asked.

"Oh, please forgive me," the lieutenant said. "I'm Jim Anderson, I am—"

"You are Martin's brother-in-law," Allison said quickly. "Martin spoke of you often. Can I get you some tea? Or coffee?"

"No, thank you," Jim said. "I'm afraid I only have a few minutes. My ship leaves France tomorrow, and I must be back there immediately. By luck I found out there was a courier plane coming to Wimbleshoe and another returning tonight. So I hopped a flight, and here I am. I . . . I just had to see you, that's all."

"I see," Allison said, hedging a little.

Jim smiled. "Don't be nervous," he said. "I'm not passing judgment or anything like that . . . If I were passing judgment, let me tell you that you would have already passed."

"Thank you," Allison said.

"I thought you might want these," Jim said, handing a package of letters to Allison.

"What are these?"

"They are your letters to him and a couple of letters he had written to you, but hadn't yet mailed. Uh, there is also a letter he was writing to Yolinda to tell her about you, but didn't finish."

Allison looked at the packet of letters, and her eyes filled with tears.

"He loved you very much, Allison," Jim went on. "And I just wanted to come by . . . to give you some sort of supportive contact with the family. I know your position hasn't been an easy one."

"No," Allison said, smiling through her tears. "No, it hasn't been easy at all."

"I'll be taking Martin home," Jim said. "I'm sorry we can't come through here. I guess your only contact with him is through me. It's a poor substitute, I know, but it's the only thing I could think of."

Allison moved across the room and into Jim's arms. Jim cushioned her head on his shoulders as she cried softly. Finally, after a long moment, Allison pulled away and looked up at him.

"You are a dear, dear man to think of this," she said. "I shall never forget you for it. Thank you, Jim. Thank you so very much."

Allison stood there for several moments after Jim left, then heard the tap, tap, tapping of Gregory's cane as he came into the room with her.

"I overheard," he said. "I thought it would be best if I stayed out of the picture until he was gone."

"Nonsense, Greg. You would have been more than welcome."

Greg smiled a slow, sad smile. "No," he said. "If I've learned anything in the month that I have been back, it is that I'm not yet ready to share time

314

with Martin . . . Nor am I ready to rush you into putting your memories of him aside. I much prefer to stay on the sidelines and wait."

"Greg, I don't want you to be hurt anymore," Allison said. "I have Martin's baby and Martin's memory to sustain me. There may be nothing for you to wait for."

"I know," Greg said. "But it is a fine thing to hope, don't you think?"

THE FIRST BIG NOVEL IN THE FIVE-BOOK MINI-SERIES, *THE WAR-TORN*

The Brave and the Lonely
by Robert Vaughan

In 1941, Hitler's unstoppable Blitzkrieg rolls across Europe, while, halfway around the world, Hirohito's war lords prepare a shattering blow against America's power in the Pacific.

Meantime, in Mount Eagle, Ill., the Holt family grows more and more aware of the global war that is to take a heartbreaking toll of all their lives.

The patriarch, Thurman Holt, who with his lovely wife, Nancy, already carries a secret sorrow, sees his children uprooted by the maelstrom.

Martin Holt, the flyer and athlete, in love with the wrong girl, will soon meet his fate, flying bomber missions over Germany . . .

Dottie Holt, pregnant and estranged from the family, follows the soldier she loves to strange and distant places . . .

Charles Holt, a youthful genius who is the conscience of the family, is recruited for a top-secret project that will have a devastating impact on the future of man on the planet . . .

SECOND IN THE *WAR-TORN* SERIES:

MASTERS AND MARTYRS

by Robert Vaughan

As the bloody drama of World War II begins, Adolph Hitler comes to Schweinfurt, vital industrial cog in the Third Reich's giant war machine.

There he meets Heinrich, head of the Rodl family, a decent man who turns away from the excesses of the Nazis—a man whose ball bearing factory is crucial to Hitler's impending Blitzkrieg.

There, the Füehrer also meets the bewitchingly beautiful Lisl Rodl, engaged to brilliant Symphony conductor, Paul Maass, whose deepest secret can destroy all those he loves.

Meantime on the eastern front, fighting a life-or-death tank battle, is Heinrich's son Rudi Rodl.

And on the other side of the world, two young Americans prepare for a fateful rendezvous with the Rodls—and history.

BE SURE TO READ THE THIRD NOVEL IN THE MINI-SERIES, *THE WAR-TORN*:

The Fallen and the Free
by Robert Vaughan

Hitler's *blitzkrieg* has come to the doorstep of the family of Marcel Garneau. The Paris cafe run by generations of Garneaus, and once favored by artists and writers such as Hemingway, Picasso and the fine French novelist, Miguel LeGrand, now echoes with the heavy jackboots of German officers.

Danger is everywhere, as Marcel's Cafe becomes a center of French underground activity, with Marcel, his lovely daughter Chantal and her lover, the same Miguel LeGrand, fighting in secret to save their honor, their lives and the doomed city of Paris.

Meanwhile, across the English Channel, Marcel's brother, Col. Georges Garneau, has escaped the disaster of Dunkirk, fallen in love with a beautiful Englishwoman, and is racing against time, against huge obstacles, with one Gen. Charles De Gaulle, to join the Allied invasion of France and rescue Paris and its people.

FOURTH IN THE *WAR-TORN* SERIES:

THE DIVINE AND THE DAMNED
by Robert Vaughan

Commander Saburo Saito, a high-born samurai of divine orign, lives with his exquisite wife, Miko, and their teen-age son, Yutake, in the city of Hiroshima. While Saburo plays a key role in the war and the son trains as a kamikaze pilot, Miko becomes involved in a secret romantic intrigue with a European diplomat that can destroy their world.

Meantime, in America, the young scientist, Charles Holt, defends the rights of loyal Japanese-Americans, and we witness the private agony of lovely Yukari Amano and the man she loves, locked up in an internment camp as a wave of hate sweeps the embattled nation.

The fate of the Saito family and their American counterparts brings them together in the fiery climax of Hiroshima.

Author Robert Vaughan talks about himself and wars he has known

I was born November 22, 1937 in Morley, Missouri, a tiny settlement on the Missouri side of the Mississippi River, just across from the location of the fictional town of Mount Eagle, Illinois (the hometown of the Holt family in *The Brave and The Lonely*).

I grew up in Sikeston, Missouri, a somewhat larger community, and, as a boy during the war, I watched the trains pass through loaded with soldiers, trucks, guns and tanks. I also remember the scrapmetal drives, the newspaper collections, ration points and air raid blackout drills.

When my father was drafted we followed him to army bases in Arkansas, Alabama and Oklahoma, before he went overseas. Thus, I was exposed to army camp life, particularly the housing shortage, to say nothing of the money shortage of an enlisted man's family.

I joined the army in the middle of the 1950s, entering army aviation, where I became a Warrant Officer, flying helicopters. I served, or traveled in, 30 countries, including Germany, France, England and Japan. Because of my interest in history, I studied the war in those countries, including visits to the libraries and archives, and had lengthy conversations with the people.

When the war heated up in Vietnam, I went over for my first tour in the early part of 1966. I flew helicopter recovery missions during this period, and over the next 18 months I saw a great deal of combat.

The most hazardous operation I participated in was one called *Junction City*, a major search and destroy operation. Near an area called "The Iron Triangle" I was part of a 13-ship element. Eight of those ships were shot down, and, as recovery officer, I had to recover each of them. It was for this mission that I was awarded the Distinguished Flying Cross. During my tours in Vietnam, I also received the Purple Heart, the Bronze Star, the Air Medal with several oak-leaf clusters, the Meritorious Service Medal, the Army Commendation Medal, the Vietnamese Cross of Gallantry, and several, lesser awards. I served eighteen months during my first tour and eighteen months on a later tour, for a total of three years in Vietnam.

My early writing reflected my military background. My first novel was a story of the U.S. Army along the DMZ in Korea. I have also done three books about Vietnam: *Brandywine's War*, *The Valkyrie Mandate*, and, under a pseudonym, *Junglefire*. Over 9,000,000 copies of my books are in print, most of them under various pen names.

I played football in my younger days, and I love all sports. I am now quite active as a football and track and field coach in Sikeston, Missouri, where I live with my wife, Ruth Ellen, and young sons, Joe and Tom.